She saw her own surprise and confusion and something else reflected in his eyes. She was too close. She stumbled back, but his hands shot out, and before she realized what was happening he was pulling her back against him, wrapping his arms around her and crashing his mouth down on hers.

Her hands found their way to his back and her fingers bunched the fabric of his jacket, itching to delve underneath to touch his skin everywhere. The hard length of his erection pressed against her stomach. His hand curved round to brush the side of her breast and she moaned into his mouth.

She froze. The sound of her own desperate longing brought her thundering back to reality. What on earth were they doing? Locked together, kissing frantically, about to rip each other's clothes off. In the lobby of a five-star hotel.

An identical thought had obviously occurred to Luke at exactly the same time. His hands stilled and he pulled back, staring down at her, his eyes so dark they were almost black and his breathing ragged as he struggled to get his body back under control.

"Oh, dear," he said huskily, letting her go, turning on his heel and striding out of the hotel.

Dear Reader,

Dramatic, passionate stories; charismatic, masterful heroes; wealth and glamour; stunning international locations—everything we love about Presents! Now two books a month are all that you expect from Presents, but with a sassy, sexy, flirty attitude!

All year you'll find these exciting new books from an array of vibrant, sparkling authors such as Kate Hardy, Heidi Rice, Kimberly Lang, Natalie Anderson and Robyn Grady. This month, Kate Hardy's *Temporary Boss, Permanent Mistress* fizzes with sparky sensual tension between a billionaire shipping tycoon and his feisty senior lawyer, Lydia. And in *Bought: Damsel in Distress,* a debut by Lucy King, heroine Emily Marchmont finds her sister has put her up for auction on the internet! Soon she's on a private jet heading for a sizzling date with the highest bidder! Luckily he's the sexiest man she's ever met....

Next month there's more sizzle and sass from talented Atlanta author Kimberly Lang with *Magnate's Mistress...Accidentally Pregnant!* And for sun, sea and sex, don't miss *Marriage: For Business or Pleasure?* by Australian author Nicola Marsh.

We'd love to hear what you think of these novels; why not drop us a line at Presents@hmb.co.uk.

With best wishes,

The Editors

Lucy King

BOUGHT: DAMSEL IN DISTRESS

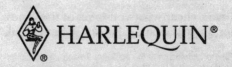

HARLEQUIN®

TORONTO • NEW YORK • LONDON
AMSTERDAM • PARIS • SYDNEY • HAMBURG
STOCKHOLM • ATHENS • TOKYO • MILAN • MADRID
PRAGUE • WARSAW • BUDAPEST • AUCKLAND

ISBN-13: 978-0-373-12890-7

BOUGHT: DAMSEL IN DISTRESS

First North American Publication 2010.

Copyright © 2009 by Lucy King.

www.eHarlequin.com

Printed in U.S.A.

All about the author...
Lucy King

LUCY KING spent her formative years lost in the world of romance novels when she really ought to have been paying attention to her teachers. Up against sparkling heroines, gorgeous heroes and the magic of falling in love, trigonometry and absolute ablatives didn't stand a chance.

But, as she couldn't live in a dreamworld forever, she eventually acquired a degree in languages and an eclectic collection of jobs. A stroll to the river Thames one Saturday morning led her to her very own hero. The minute she laid eyes on the hunky rower getting out of a boat, clad only in Lycra® and carrying a three-meter oar as if it were a toothpick, she knew she'd met the man she was going to marry. Luckily the rower thought the same.

She will always be grateful to whatever it was that made her stop dithering and actually sit down to type Chapter One, because dreaming up her own sparkling heroines and gorgeous heroes is pretty much her idea of the perfect job.

Originally a Londoner, Lucy now lives in Spain, where she spends much of her time reading, failing to finish cryptic crosswords and trying to convince herself that lying on the beach really is the best way to work.

To my family, for their unfailing support.

CHAPTER ONE

'YOU must be wondering what sort of girl ends up for auction on the internet,' said Emily, picking up her glass of champagne and taking a quick sip. If she'd known such a course of action would lead to being swept off to the south of France by a gorgeous man in his private jet she'd have done it years ago, and to hell with what sort of girl it made her.

'The thought had crossed my mind,' Luke replied. He reached for his briefcase and flicked open the catches.

Emily settled back into the beige leather seat and looked out of the window, down at the fields and towns outside London as they blurred into ever smaller smudges of grey and green. 'What conclusions did you draw?' she said distractedly.

'I couldn't possibly comment.'

'That bad?' Was he being serious? Emily stifled a tiny sigh of defeat. Trying not to stare at the handsome face, broad shoulders and lean body of the man sitting diagonally opposite her, trying not to ogle the big tanned hands extracting a report from a folder, wasn't working. It was like struggling to ignore the pull of a very strong magnet. Impossible. Her eyes swivelled to the dark head bent over the papers.

'Unrepeatable,' he replied, glancing up at her.

There went her stomach again. Slowly flipping over at the combination of eyes the colour of the Mediterranean in summer, the sexy half-smile and the deep, rumbling voice. Swooping in a way that had nothing to do with the flight.

Emily wrinkled her nose. 'I can imagine. I'd have run through Lonely to Loopy with a stop-off at Desperate on the way. Not that I am any of those, of course,' she added hastily.

'Of course not,' he said, in a tone that suggested he thought just that. 'How did you guess?'

Ooooh, *ouch*. 'I simply imagined what sort of person would respond to an ad like that,' she replied sweetly.

Luke sat back and fixed her with a coolly amused stare. 'I see you've regained the power of speech. It's back with a bite.'

Emily fought the urge to squirm under his penetrating gaze and gave him what she thought might look like an apologetic smile. 'Today has taken on an unexpectedly surreal quality. I'm only just getting my head round it.'

The moment they'd met, the instant she'd put her hand in his to shake it, she'd been struck uncharacteristically dumb. Her body had felt as though it had received a thousand-volt charge. Her heart had jumped and she'd gone momentarily dizzy, the blood racing to parts of her body that had been out of action for so long she'd forgotten she had them. She'd never experienced sexual attraction like it, and it was making her feel slightly unhinged.

'You don't invite strange men to transport you to foreign countries often?' he asked, tilting his head to one side.

'I don't invite strange men to transport me anywhere ever.'

'In that case why are you here?'

Emily shuddered. 'You met my sister.'

He nodded. 'A formidable woman.'

He sounded as if he thought this was an admirable quality. Emily frowned and pinched the bridge of her nose. 'You have *no* idea.'

Four hours earlier

'You did *what*?' Emily nearly dropped her muffin into her cappuccino as her head snapped up and she gaped at her sister.

'I said I sold you. On the internet.' Anna glanced at her watch and then wiped her sons' faces.

Emily felt a sliver of concern and raked her gaze over her sister's immaculate exterior. Had she gone mad? Anna certainly looked normal, but who knew what could be lurking beneath the surface? If this was what motherhood did to a previously perfectly intelligent, clear-thinking woman then she was glad she'd made the decision never to have children herself.

She nodded as if in understanding. 'Right. You sold me. On the internet. Aren't there laws against things like that?'

'Apparently not. It was surprisingly easy,' replied Anna, calmly folding the tissue and placing it on her empty plate.

'You are joking, aren't you?'

Anna fixed Emily with a stern stare. 'Not at all. I'm deadly serious.'

It was a look Emily was very familiar with. As realisation dawned, her smile slipped from her face. 'Oh, my God. You *are* serious.'

'Of course. I wouldn't joke about a thing like this.'

Emily began to hyperventilate.

'Now, don't get hysterical,' said Anna, thrusting a glass of water into her hand. 'Deep breaths… If it makes you feel any better, I didn't exactly sell *you*.'

Emily flapped her other hand in front of her face and fought for breath. 'So what did you sell?' she said, when she was finally able to speak.

Anna shrugged. 'A once-in-a-lifetime opportunity. In this age of equality, a chance to be chivalrous. The rescue of a damsel in distress.'

What? Since when had her sister developed a romantic streak? 'And I'm the damsel?'

Anna nodded.

'But why would you do that?' Emily asked, utterly bewildered. 'I'm not in distress.'

'You are. The French baggage handlers are on strike.'

Oh, no, not this again.

'Don't look at me like that,' said Anna indignantly. 'Your obstinate refusal to go to Tom's wedding is not healthy. You haven't been out for so much as a drink with anyone since you split up. That's not a single date in over a year. You need closure, and you're not going to get it until you see the rat safely hitched to some other poor woman. Then you'll be able to move on.'

'He may have dumped me and got engaged to an aristocratic French floozy two months later, but he's not a rat,' said Emily wearily, ignoring the sceptical look Anna threw her. 'And for the millionth time I *have* moved on.'

Anna glanced at her watch. 'Talking of moving on, we need to go home.' She turned, and with an imperceptible nod of her head signalled for the bill.

'Why?' Emily said carefully, tendrils of suspicion winding round her nerves.

'Because the person who won the auction is turning up at any minute.'

Emily gaped in horror. 'What? *Now*?'

'Of course,' Anna replied, standing up and brushing a crumb off her front. 'The wedding is tomorrow, isn't it?'

Emily could only nod in dumb stupefaction.

'Well, then. You leave this afternoon.' Anna marched to the bar to pay, leaving Emily to unravel the chaos of the last five minutes. But it was all too much. Where did she start?

'Who won?' she managed eventually as they started along the path that led across the common to Anna's house.

'A man called Luke Harrison. He was very determined. The bidding went right to the wire. It was gripping stuff, I can tell you.'

'I'm so glad.' Emily's sarcastic tone went unnoticed.

'So was I. *greatsexguaranteed* was also extremely persistent, but I had a funny feeling about him.'

'Can't think why. So how is this Luke Harrison going to

help me get to France?' Emily panted, struggling to keep up with Anna's brutal pace.

'Private jet. Rather inspired, I thought.'

'But I have plans this weekend. I can't just drop everything.'

Anna shot her a sceptical look. 'A pot that urgently needs glazing?'

Emily bit her lip and nodded.

'You're twenty-eight. You should be Out There. Meeting men. Not hunched over a wheel with clay under your nails. Pots won't keep you warm at night.'

Emily glared at Anna mutinously. 'I have an electric blanket.'

Anna marched on, undeterred.

Emily tried again. 'How do you know he's got a plane? How do you know he's going to turn up? He might be a lunatic. I mean, what sort of person bids for a woman in an internet auction? He could be a kidnapper, a murderer—anyone.' Her voice was rising, becoming more desperate. Anna merely looked at her witheringly and Emily threw her hands up in exasperation. 'You're insane.'

'I'm a genius. Don't be so melodramatic. I spoke to his mother on the phone and discovered that we have friends in common.'

Emily's jaw dropped. 'His mother?'

'I had to get references,' said Anna defensively. 'You don't think I'd send you off with just anyone, do you?'

'I am suddenly at a complete loss as to *what* you would do.'

'I've arranged for him to pick you up here so that we can check him out first. Just in case.'

Emily ground her teeth. 'It'll be a wasted journey. I'm not going.'

Anna stopped at the bottom of the steps leading up to her front door and rummaged in her bag for the keys. 'Think of the charity.'

Emily's eyes narrowed. 'What charity?'

'The money Mr Harrison paid is going to a charity that investigates and helps prevent maternal mortality.'

Emily gasped. A familiar dull pain clenched her heart and she felt the blood drain from her face. 'That's a low blow, Anna,' she said quietly.

'It's not meant to be, darling. But I spent years bringing you up and I hate to see you wasting your life over that loser. Will you do it for me?'

Emily wavered. She owed her sister so much. Anna had made huge sacrifices on her behalf. When their father had died, fourteen years after their mother, it had been left to Anna to raise her. And she knew she hadn't been the easiest of teenagers to handle. Besides, her sister in this mode was unstoppable, and there was only so much battering she could take. Her resistance crumbled and she let out a resigned sigh. 'OK. Assuming he's not crazy, or worse, I'll go. Can I take David with me?'

'No husband borrowing. Besides, he's at a conference in New York.'

Emily straightened her spine. 'Fine. I'll just have to enter the lion's den single and strong and shod in killer heels.'

'They're already packed.'

Emily raised an eyebrow. 'How ruthlessly efficient.'

Anna inclined her head. 'Thank you.'

'It's not a compliment.'

But Anna wasn't paying attention. She was staring over Emily's shoulder, and her expression became dreamy. 'I think this might be him. Bang on time too.'

Emily turned to look at the man striding towards them. He was tall, broad-shouldered and very good-looking, and a dart of awareness shivered through her. 'If it is,' she murmured, watching the sun glinting off his dark hair, 'I may just forgive you.'

After that her composure had taken such a hammering she couldn't really remember what had happened. Her sensible court-shoe-wearing sister had batted her eyelashes and giggled her way through some very rudimentary questions about his integrity and his intentions, had established that Luke Harrison was single, solvent, and in possession of a plane, and had then bundled Emily into his car without so much as a backward glance. Was it any wonder that she'd been unable to formulate a sensible sentence throughout the journey to the airport?

'So, why are you here?'

Luke's voice jerked her out of her reverie. 'Oh, er—' She stopped. She could hardly tell him the truth. Revealing that she was heading to her ex-fiancé's wedding to another woman would rather negate her earlier declaration that she was neither lonely nor desperate. 'A friend's getting married near Nice, and Anna was under the misapprehension that I wanted to go to the wedding.'

'Scheduled airlines a little pedestrian?'

Emily bristled. 'Of course a man who has a private plane wouldn't know about anything as trivial as industrial action, but for us mere mortals a baggage handlers' strike does tend to put a spanner in the works.'

Luke had the grace to look a little apologetic. Only fleetingly, but it was enough to mollify her. 'The only flights that weren't cancelled were full. Which suited me fine.' Emily twiddled a lock of hair around her finger. 'I have better things to do with my weekend than go to a wedding I don't want to attend.'

'Why didn't you say so earlier? I could have dropped you home on the way to the airport.'

'I did think about it, but Anna probably has her spies ready and waiting in France, primed to report back on my every move from the moment I arrive. You saw her earlier. She'd broken into my house to pack and pick up my passport. She didn't tell me that she'd put me up for auction until about half an hour before you showed up, and even then she deliberately waited until we were in a public place so I couldn't throttle her.' Not to mention the emotional blackmail that Anna had deployed with such success. Emily sighed. 'She's utterly devious. It's not worth the grief. I'll just have to grin and bear it and count down the hours until you take me back.'

'She went to a hell of an effort so that you could attend this wedding. Why would she do that if she knew you didn't want to go?'

Emily shrugged evasively. Those blue eyes of his were far too probing for her comfort. 'Beats me. Before she went on maternity leave she used to troubleshoot for one of the big accountancy firms. I think she's been missing the challenge. Do you have siblings?'

'No. I do, however, have relatives with an over-zealous interest in my well-being, so I can sympathise.'

'Perhaps they should meet. We could cast them into a parallel universe where they're forced to watch reality TV on a ten-minute loop for all eternity.'

One corner of Luke's mouth lifted and Emily was instantly transfixed by the movement. What did his lips feel like? she wondered. Soft or firm? What would they feel like moving over hers? Her own mouth tingled at the thought and her pulse leapt. An image of him tugging her into his arms, plastering her up against that hard body, kissing her senseless slammed into her head, making her dizzy and breathless. Then she noticed his smile fading. When she looked up his face was blank, but his eyes had darkened to indigo.

Something resembling irritation flashed across his face. Emily swallowed and tried to get a grip. 'So, what exactly did the advert say?'

'It offered a once-in-a-lifetime opportunity to be a knight in shining armour. The chance to rescue a damsel in distress. And mentioned the more prosaic need for a plane, a passport and a free weekend.'

Emily bit her lip and nodded. Then she frowned. 'That's it?'

'There was a photo.'

She went cold. 'A photo?' Oh, God. 'Which one?'

'You were on a beach.'

Emily went even colder. Please, no. She took a deep breath. 'Green bikini?'

'That's the one.'

Freezing to red hot in under a second. It had to be a record, she thought, as her cheeks burned. If it was the picture she was thinking of, she was wearing a green rather-on-the-small-side bikini. In fact, she wasn't so much wearing it as falling out of it. 'I'm going to kill her,' she muttered.

'Why?'

'Why?' she spluttered. Oh, the humiliation.

'You had over a hundred people bidding for you.'

'Really?' Emily's pride swelled for a moment, before mortification squashed it. She dropped her head in her hands. 'How could she do that?' she mumbled. 'Of all the photos… I don't know why she didn't just put a flyer in a phone box and be done with it.'

Luke laughed and the sound rumbled right through her, scrambling her brain momentarily.

'Dare I ask which category she put me in?'

'Are you sure you want to know?'

'Not entirely. But you might as well complete my humiliation.'

'Collectibles. Decorative Objects.'

Emily groaned. It went from bad to worse. How long could she stay there with her head buried in her hands? For ever? At some point she'd have to look up. Denial, that was the thing. Generally she wasn't a fan of denial, but this was an exceptional circumstance.

Fixing a neutral expression on her face, Emily lifted her head and shot him a curious glance. 'Why did you bid?'

Luke went still and his gaze dropped to his papers. Then he shrugged. 'To be honest, I'm not sure.'

A flicker of something that Emily couldn't identify passed over his face. Whatever his motives had been, like her, he wasn't sharing. 'A rash impulse?' she suggested helpfully, when no further answer seemed forthcoming.

Luke sat back and looked at her, that faint smile still playing around his mouth and doing all sorts of strange, fluttery things to her stomach.

'Maybe it appealed to my adventurous side.'

Emily considered this. Adventurous? For a man who must regularly fly by private jet? She shook her head. 'Nope, sorry, I'm sticking with the rash impulse.'

'Maybe I was intrigued by the idea of being a knight in shining armour.'

Right. Sure. She didn't believe that for a second either. 'With a plane instead of a horse?'

'A suit instead of the armour.'

'Same thing sometimes,' she batted back.

He tilted his head and regarded her thoughtfully. 'Very true,' he said finally.

'With a laptop instead of a lance,' she added, tapping a finger against her mouth. 'Of course, no real knight would be anything without a castle.'

Luke rubbed his jaw. 'A castle?'

'At the very least. A palace would be ideal.'

'Would a penthouse in Mayfair do instead?'

She pretended to give it some consideration. 'Lots of chrome and steel and glass and thoroughly pointless gadgets?'

Luke nodded. 'Goes without saying.'

'In that case, congratulations. You're really rather well-qualified for the role of knight.'

'Thank you. How well-suited are you to being a damsel in distress?'

'Not well at all, I'm afraid,' she said with a rueful smile. 'No flowing locks and no ivory tower.'

'No evil father and wicked stepmother either, I hope.' Amusement glinted in his eyes.

'No parents at all,' she said evenly.

The amusement faded. 'I'm sorry.'

Emily shrugged. 'Don't be. They died a long time ago.' The lightness of her tone belied the clench of her heart. She knew it did. She'd spent years perfecting it. Swallowing down the lump that had lodged in her throat, she gave him a bright smile. 'So, knights in shining armour aside, do you often look for women on the internet?'

From the scowl that appeared on his face, Emily deduced that he didn't appreciate what she was implying. 'Sorry,' she said, flushing slightly. 'That didn't come out quite the way I expected.'

Luke picked up his pen and uncapped it. 'It's an inevitable assumption. But, no, I don't trawl the internet looking for women.'

Of course he didn't, she mused. He probably had women tripping over themselves to appear on his arm. He clearly hadn't entered into the bidding war because he'd been overwhelmed by her curves.

'A friend of mine e-mailed me the link. I was going to Nice anyway. I was curious.'

Bizarre. It was bizarre enough to be true. She hardly knew him. It might be exactly the sort of thing he would do. How did she know?

'Just out of interest, how much did I fetch?'

He smiled suddenly at her, and her breath caught. 'Do you want it in dollars, euros or pounds? It's a global market out there, you know.'

She couldn't help smiling back. 'An estimate will do.'

'Around six figures.'

Emily nearly knocked over her glass.

'Are you mad?'

His jaw tightened. 'Very possibly.'

A tiny trickle of ice shivered down her spine at his tone. He wasn't joking. Emily stared at him as he raked a hand through his hair and yanked open the top button of his shirt. On a plane with a madman, however gorgeous, was not top of her list of ideal scenarios and if he'd said 'yes' instead of 'possibly' she'd be reaching for the nearest parachute. 'At least it's tax deductible.'

'There is that,' he agreed.

'Why are you going to Nice?'

'Meetings in Monte Carlo.'

She tilted her head. 'Convenient.'

'You don't believe me.'

Emily shot him an assessing glance. 'I'm not sure.'

He clutched his chest as if in pain. 'I'm wounded.'

'I'm devastated that you're wounded.'

'You should be. Your sister accepted my reasons without question.'

Did she? Emily's eyes narrowed. 'My sister's brain has been pulverised by motherhood,' she said darkly.

'You're more wary?'

'Maybe,' she murmured, wrenching her eyes from his and looking down at where her fingers were playing with the ends of the scarf tied round her head.

That particular avenue of conversation was not one she wanted to pursue. Weaving the strands between her fingers, she found herself wondering whether it was true. She'd spent hours analysing her relationship with Tom and what had gone wrong, but she hadn't looked at the effects it had left behind.

She probably had become more wary since breaking up with him, she acknowledged, her brow creasing. Five years with the same man was a long time, even if the last year had been pretty rocky, and her dating skills were rusty. Plus, she thought she'd known her ex-fiancé inside out, and it turned out she hadn't known him at all.

Perhaps Anna was right. Perhaps she did need closure. It wasn't normal for a girl of twenty-eight to hang up her dating shoes. She did need to get Out There.

At least her reaction to Luke proved that she was still capable of feeling sexual desire. Emily stole a peek at him from beneath her lashes just to make sure that it was still there. He was reading a report with amazing speed, underlining sections, writing notes, his long fingers flicking though the pages, almost *caressing* the paper. Oh, yes, sexual desire was definitely still there, if the bolt of fire that spread through her was any proof. Her gaze slid up to where a wedge of chest was exposed by the open collar of his shirt. Her focus zoomed in on the fine dark hairs that emerged from the bottom of the V, and she had to ball her hands into fists to stop her fingers whipping up and ripping open another couple of buttons.

'I can't concentrate on my report if you keep staring at me like that.'

Emily froze. Oh, God. He was watching her watching him! Had she been caught in the act? How excruciating. She tentatively lifted her gaze further, fully expecting to see a mocking glint in his eyes, but he was still looking down. That was even worse: he'd been able to *feel* her eyes devouring him. She went crimson and clapped her hands to her cheeks, turning an involuntary groan of shame into a lengthy cough.

'Would you like some water?' he enquired mildly, still apparently absorbed.

She cleared her throat. 'Yes, but don't worry. I'll get it.' Standing up and moving around would do her good. It might even give her body the opportunity to redistribute her blood away from her face. 'I wouldn't want your concentration to be disturbed any further,' she added, levering herself out of the seat.

She wandered across the cream carpet towards the drinks cabinet where Luke had poured her champagne when they'd boarded. What a way to travel. No interminable check-in queues, no stuffing your case into an overfilled overhead locker and yourself into an uncomfortable seat. And a travelling companion that looked like Luke. Her skin prickled and she went warm.

'Would you like anything?' she asked, taking a bottle of water out of the fridge and filling a glass. She pressed the cold bottle against her cheek and felt it cool her overheated body.

Sticking a hand in the back pocket of her jeans, she took a sip and bent down to look out of the window at the great expanse of azure sky.

'No, thanks. And you're disturbing me.'

Emily blinked, instantly aware that her skin had prickled, was still tingling, because his eyes had been burning into her back. 'No, I'm not,' she said calmly. 'You're watching me.'

A pause, and then, 'Like I said, you're disturbing me.'

CHAPTER TWO

EMILY went still while her body temperature rocketed. Had he really just said that? Did it mean what she thought it meant? She straightened and turned, eyes wide, not quite sure what to say next.

Luke wasn't in his seat. He'd moved to the fax machine and was shuffling the pages into the feeder. What with the hum of the engines and the thickness of the carpet she hadn't heard him move.

She took a deep breath. 'Am I?' she said.

Luke didn't break from what he was doing. 'Are you what?'

'Disturbing you?'

'Not at all,' he said, whipping round and flashing her a brief smile. 'Make yourself at home. Help yourself to anything you like.'

What?

Then she shrugged. She must have misunderstood, she decided, following his movements over the rim of her glass as he strode back to the chair. He picked up his own glass and tossed the contents down his throat. Emily slid back into her seat and watched him as he leaned and twisted over to pull out another report. The muscles in his torso were clearly defined beneath his shirt. He pushed up his sleeves to reveal strong, tanned forearms and her mouth went dry.

Emily didn't generally have a thing about forearms, but

Luke's were—well, they were making her reconsider. Tanned, muscled, lightly sprinkled with rough hair. She felt a fierce urge to run her hands over them. Her eyes fell to the long brown fingers idly twirling the pen as he concentrated on the report. Compared to the speed with which he'd read the last document, this one seemed hard going. In fact, he hadn't turned the page once, and he hadn't underlined a single word or made any notes whatsoever. If pressed, she'd have sworn he was distracted.

She would do the decent thing and rescue him from his torturous report by dazzling him with her conversational skills. But before she could make a start on finding out what made this enticingly enigmatic man tick, Luke shot to his feet and went to pour himself some more water.

'Don't you drink?' she asked when he returned. She'd been merrily sipping away at her champagne since take-off, but he hadn't touched a drop.

'Not on a Friday when I've got meetings in the afternoon.'

She nodded sagely. 'Very wise. On the other hand, who arranges meetings on a Friday afternoon? It's practically the weekend.'

'I have clients in Monte Carlo. And it's not the weekend.'

Mmm. 'What do you do?'

'I'm a fund manager.'

'Ah, interesting.'

Luke smiled. 'Not really. Unless you happen to have an obsession with derivatives and index futures.'

'Which you do?'

'I seem to have a knack for making money out of them.'

And didn't that neatly avoid the question? She nodded in what she hoped was a knowledgeable fashion. 'I should imagine there are quite a few high net worth individuals in Monte Carlo.'

Luke's eyebrows shot up. 'You know about high net worth individuals?'

'Don't sound so surprised. I know a little about lots of things.'

'Like what?' He linked his hands together and leaned forward.

'Like how City boys like you can spend ten thousand pounds on a gold leaf cocktail,' she said, giving him a small smile to show she was half joking.

Luke frowned. 'A few do. I don't. And nor do any of my staff. They don't have time. Plus, they know they'd be fired if they did.'

She shuddered. Ruthless as well as gorgeous. A dangerously attractive combination.

He shot her a sudden killer smile that had her blood racing round her body. 'Besides, I prefer to spend my money on rescuing damsels.'

'You mean there are others?' she said, trying not to sound too curious.

'Not at the moment. It's very distressing.'

Emily let out a burst of laughter.

'What about you? What do you do?'

'A bit of this, a bit of that.' Emily smiled at the quizzical look on his face. 'I'm a professional temp, currently resting.' She waited. This was the moment when people usually scoffed at her, or told her what an idiot she was for not pursuing a proper career.

Luke leaned back. 'What made you choose to be a temp?'

Emily was taken aback. He sounded genuinely interested. Most people assumed that she was temping until she could find a proper job. Whereas she'd made a deliberate decision to make it a career. 'I like the flexibility. Days off when I want. It's perfect. It gives me time to do the things I love doing.'

He was looking at her as though she was speaking in a foreign language. 'Such as?'

'Spending time with my sister and her twins. Seeing friends, potting, that kind of thing.'

'Potting?'

'Potting. Making pots.'

'Are you any good?'

'No idea. But I don't have to be. It's a hobby. I do it for fun.' That wasn't strictly true. She'd love to make a living out of it, but she suspected she wasn't much good. 'Temping is really just a way of paying the bills. Funnily enough, I once worked at a fund manager's.'

'Oh? Which one?'

'JT Investments. Do you know it?'

Luke nodded. 'I know the CEO.'

'Jack Taylor? I never met him, but the work was interesting. Challenging.' She shrugged. 'That's what I mean. I like the variety of the work. Meeting new people, discovering new gossip without any need to get involved in office politics. And then, just when you start thinking it's getting a tad monotonous—which, let's face it, most jobs are—you get to leave and try something else. It's great.' She grinned at him. He still wasn't getting it, but that was all right, most people didn't. She leaned forward. 'Are you sure you don't want to give me a lecture on the folly of my decision? About how unstable temping is, and how my brain must be atrophying, and that at my age I really should be sprinting up a career ladder?'

'Why would I do that? You clearly enjoy what you do.' He frowned slightly at this, as if it was an unfamiliar concept to him. 'And it's none of my business.'

Emily sniffed. 'That doesn't stop most people.'

He looked at her thoughtfully. 'I know… I've been on the receiving end of something similar.'

'Really?'

Something in his voice—bitterness, weariness, maybe—had her senses leaping to attention. 'What would people lecture you about, I wonder?' she said.

In the long silent seconds while he regarded her, Emily's heart began to beat faster.

'Apparently I need more fun in my life,' he said eventually, his tone leaving her in no doubt about what he thought of that piece of advice. 'Apparently I work too hard.'

'Do you?'

'Perhaps.'

'Why?' she asked, suddenly feeling that she was entering into choppy water.

'Habit,' he said flatly.

'What do you do to relax?'

'Relax?' His brows snapped together.

'Yes, you know. Relax. Chill out, unwind.'

'I don't have time to relax.'

Okaaayyy. 'What about the fun part?'

His eyes glittered. 'If I needed fun in my life,' he said, his voice rumbling over her, 'I'd be perfectly capable of finding it.'

The way he was looking at her, his gaze scorching over her face before resting on her mouth, set her blood to boiling. His eyes had turned the colour of the sky at midnight and his expression shifted, darkened, intensified—as if there was only one thing on his mind. Then it vanished and his face was impassive once again.

But Emily had caught it. She *hadn't* been mistaken about what exactly it was that had been disturbing him earlier.

For that brief moment Luke had considered finding fun with *her.*

Her heart pounded and her ears popped. The problem was, she mused, as the pilot's voice advised them they were starting their descent, that once they'd landed and gone their separate ways there wasn't anything that could be done about it.

He should have left her at the bloody airport, thought Luke grimly, handing the porter a crisp note and watching him disappear with Emily's suitcase.

That would have been the sensible, logical, rational thing to do. It was a shame, then, that sense, logic and reason had taken a hike hours ago.

'Are you sure this is the right place?' Emily was squinting up at the hotel and rocking on her heels.

'Yes,' he said curtly. Her sister had booked her into the one of the oldest, most exclusive hotels on the coast.

'But look at the place,' she wailed. 'And look at me.'

Against his better judgement, he did as she suggested. He ran his gaze over her profile. Wavy fair hair was held back in a wide scarf, the ends of which dangled down her back. She was wearing a close fitting pink T-shirt and well-worn jeans that hugged the curve of her bottom. He felt a savage kick of desire in the pit of his stomach as he followed the long line of her legs to where fuchsia-painted toenails were peeping out of some sort of high-heeled shoe.

'They'll never let me in in jeans—and non-designer ones at that.'

'You have a room booked for two nights at five hundred euros a night,' Luke said tersely. 'They're not going to question what you're wearing.'

Emily swivelled to face him, her jaw dropping. 'Five hundred euros? A night?'

'A night,' he confirmed, grabbing her elbow and leading her into the lobby. 'You'd better make the most of it.'

'I shall,' she said, flashing him a wicked smile. The sooner he got out of here the better. 'I'll raid the mini bar and download dozens of saucy films, and then Anna will rue the day she decided to auction me off to the highest bidder.'

Saucy films? Luke's jaw clenched. His fingers tightened and he quickened his pace. He needed to leave. Now. Before he succumbed to the demands his body had been making since the moment he'd laid eyes on her.

He propelled her across the lobby, deposited her at the reception desk, and took a step back. For a second he just stared at her, his mind suddenly blank. Then he noticed that her mouth, that highly distracting mouth, was moving. He forced his attention to what she was saying.

'Thank you for the lift,' she said, smiling faintly.

'You're welcome. It was on my way anyway. Have a good weekend.'

A shadow flickered across her face, clouding her eyes. 'I'll try. You too.'

Luke gave her a brief nod, turned on his heel and strode towards the door. With every step he felt the return of his focus. Hell, not just his focus. His sanity. Ever since he'd clicked on that damn link that Jack had sent him and seen her photo he'd been steadily losing it. Lusting over her picture as if he was a hormonal adolescent instead of the cool, disciplined, rock-steady man he had made himself become. For a man who liked to be in control, the last few hours had been a harrowing experience.

'Luke?'

Her voice reached him when he was halfway to the door. You didn't hear that, he muttered to himself. Don't stop. Nearly there.

'Luke?'

This time her voice was closer and huskier, wrapping round the sound of his name like velvet, and it slammed him to a halt. He turned to find Emily standing a foot away from him, looking at him warily. 'Yes?'

'Would you come to this wedding with me?'

When Luke went rigid, and paled beneath his tan, Emily instantly regretted the impulse that had made her run after him. She shouldn't have asked. She knew that. It was just that as he'd walked away she'd had the oddest feeling that she'd never see him again. That somehow he'd arrange not to have to accompany her back to London on Sunday. And that she'd have to endure the torture of Tom's wedding with nothing whatsoever to look forward to.

But maybe he had plans for the weekend. She'd seen how busy he was from the endless string of phone calls that he'd juggled during the journey from the airport to the hotel. He must have piles of work to do. Why on earth would he want to waste his valuable time on her?

* * *

No. That was Luke's answer to her question. He had a stack of analyst reports and stockmarket data to get through before the weekend was over. Even if he hadn't had that excuse, he hadn't been to a wedding or inside a church in years, and he certainly wasn't about to start now. So if that was what she'd been planning all along, she'd got landed with the wrong man.

His eyes narrowed as he watched her, standing there waiting for his answer, fiddling with her hair, her green eyes shining steadily at him. She was nibbling on her lower lip again. An arrow of heat fired through him, tightening and stiffening his body, just as it had done on the plane. He fought back a surge of desire. Emily was resourceful and confident. She'd manage fine on her own.

At the precise moment when Luke opened his mouth to tell her that he had other plans Emily jammed her hands in the back pockets of her jeans. The movement thrust her breasts forward and he lost what little sense he'd had left.

'Forget it. I—' she began.

'Sure—why not?' He cut her off, his voice thick and distant. His head throbbed with a sudden desperate urge to haul her up against him and see if she was as soft and yielding as she looked.

'Really?' Emily let out a breath and her shoulders relaxed, while Luke shoved a hand through his hair, nodded, and called himself all kinds of bloody idiot.

'Great,' she said, beaming at him. 'It might even be fun. It's at six tomorrow evening, at a château near Valensole. There's a reception and a dinner afterwards.'

Luke was looking shell-shocked. Emily was just beginning to wonder whether he'd heard her when he said, 'I'll pick you up at three.'

She looked up at him in surprise. 'Is it that far?'

'A couple of hours.'

Emily frowned. That changed things. She couldn't expect him to give up such a large chunk of his weekend. 'Are you sure you don't mind?' she asked.

He lifted an eyebrow. 'I may even be able to dig out a morning suit.'

Emily smiled, feeling happier and more settled than she had in hours. 'Thank you, Luke.'

And then, because she really was grateful, and because it seemed the natural thing to do, she reached up and planted a light kiss at the corner of his mouth.

But there was nothing natural about her reaction. The moment her mouth grazed his skin the world wobbled. Her lips tingled and his smell—clean, masculine and untainted by after-shave—swirled into her head. Sensation washed over her. Emily swayed and then jerked back, unable to stifle a tiny gasp of shock.

She saw her own surprise and confusion and something else reflected in his eyes. Her breath caught in her throat and suddenly she couldn't breathe. She was too close. The heat radiating off his body was scorching her. She stumbled back, but his hands shot out, and before she'd realised what was happening he was pulling her back against him, wrapping his arms around her and crashing his mouth down on hers.

He took advantage of her parted lips instantly, his tongue darting into her mouth and exploring her with a thoroughness that turned her bones to water. His fingers tangled in her hair, angling her head, and he deepened the kiss. Emily's heart banged around her chest and her blood raced around her body like a stream of fire.

Her own hands found their way to his back and her fingers bunched the fabric of his jacket, itching to delve underneath and touch his skin everywhere. The hard length of his erection pressed against her stomach. His hand curved round to brush the side of her breast and she moaned into his mouth.

She froze. The sound of her own desperate longing brought her thundering back to reality. What on earth were they doing? Locked together, kissing frantically, about to rip each other's clothes off. In the lobby of a five-star hotel.

An identical thought had obviously occurred to Luke at

exactly the same time. His hands stilled and he pulled back, staring down at her, his eyes so dark they were almost black, his breathing ragged as he struggled to get his body back under control.

'Oh, dear,' he said huskily, letting her go, turning on his heel and striding out of the hotel.

'That's all he said? "Oh, dear"?'

'Yes, for the tenth time, that's all he said.' Emily closed her eyes and flopped back on the bed, seriously doubting the wisdom of calling her sister in the hope that she'd be able to shed some light on the situation.

'How did he say it?'

An image of Luke's face just before he marched off floated into her head. 'Kind of neutral. Expressionless. Blank. What do you think he meant?'

'Who knows? It could be anything from *That was fantastic and I'm in danger of falling head over heels in love with this woman—*'

Emily's heart lurched for a second. 'Rather unlikely, don't you think?'

'—to *God, I pity you. Your kissing technique is diabolical.*'

Emily groaned and clapped a hand over her eyes. As far as she could remember—and she'd relived the experience a hundred times in the past hour or so—his technique had been perfect. Whether hers had been any good was anyone's guess. She'd lost her mind and any finesse the moment their mouths had met. 'I'm rather hoping it was *What the hell are we thinking of, two grown adults kissing like frenzied teenagers in a hotel lobby in full view of a dozen people?*'

'Perhaps we'll never know. How is the hotel, by the way?'

Emily sat up and surveyed her room. 'Amazing. Forget a cat, you could swing a pride of lions in here. Thank you for booking it.'

'You're welcome.'

'Guess what's on the balcony.'

'Hmm, let me think. A table? Chairs? A couple of wilting pot plants?'

'A hot tub.'

'Big enough for two?'

'Oh, yes.' Her imagination had come up with some pretty racy scenarios involving her and Luke, with little clothing and lots of bubbles. She closed her eyes and lost herself in the memory of Luke's mouth moving over hers, warm and firm, his taste, his smell, the feel of his body crushing hers…

'Remember that at the wedding. You're clearly on a roll. You might get lucky.'

'What wedding?' asked Emily dreamily.

'Er, tomorrow?' Anna's tone sharpened. 'Don't even *think* about not going. If you do, I'll cancel my credit card and you'll be landed with the hotel bill.'

Emily sat up. 'Oh, I'm going. I'm definitely going. Luke's coming with me.'

She had to hold her mobile away from her ear as her sister let out a very unlike-Anna squeal.

She frowned. 'At least that was the plan. After the "Oh, dear" episode I'm not sure whether he'll turn up.'

'Of course he will. He's a man of his word.'

'How on earth do you figure that?'

'He turned up to take you to France, didn't he? He'll be there tomorrow. And when he is, you can ask him what he meant.'

But did she want to know? That was the question that had been swirling around Emily's head for the past twenty-four hours. Their kiss had replayed in her mind all night. Her response to Luke was overwhelming. How could she react like this to a man she'd only just met and barely knew? For the first time in her life she was at the mercy of an extraordinary attraction that was as unsettling as it was exciting. This, plus the steamy thoughts generated by the discovery of a complimentary box of condoms in a bathroom cupboard, had made her toss and turn until she'd finally given up and gone to pound her restlessness out in the pool.

At least the hotel beautician had managed to cover up the worst of the grey circles under her eyes, and the hairdresser had sorted her hair out so that her feather fascinator looked as though it did actually belong where it was.

Her sister had packed well, thought Emily, slipping into the dress she'd worn to Anna and David's wedding. A dress which had earned compliments from everyone except Tom. She should have realised something wasn't quite right between the two of them way back then.

She thrust her feet into gold strappy sandals and glanced at her watch. Quarter to three. Her hands were trembling as they fumbled with the straps. The butterflies in her stomach were clamouring to escape. She wasn't sure quite what her nerves were for. The wedding, or coming face to face with Luke? Both probably.

After the way he'd walked out yesterday evening she wouldn't be at all surprised if he didn't show up this afternoon, despite Anna's assurances. Anna hadn't seen the stunned expression on his face when he'd agreed to go with her, as if he'd been as startled by his answer as she was. Nor had she seen his face darken in a way that suggested he'd regretted his decision the moment he'd made it. So if he *was* waiting for her downstairs, what mood would he be in?

Oh, well, thought Emily, there was only one way to find out. She picked up her clutch bag, pulled her shoulders back and glanced at herself in the mirror. If there was one thing she was certain of, she told herself, taking a series of deep, steadying breaths and checking her teeth for lipstick, the next few hours were going to be anything but boring.

CHAPTER THREE

FUN. Was that what this was supposed to be? Luke asked himself grimly, pushing through the hotel's revolving door and stalking across the gleaming marble floor. Fun was supposed to be light, nothing more than a passing diversion. It was not supposed to knock him for six, and it was not supposed to derail his focus to such an extent that his clients had asked him if he was all right in the middle of the meeting.

Luke scowled as he scanned the lobby in case Emily was early, and then flung himself onto the sofa, picked up the first magazine his fingers found and flicked to an article on interest rate forecasts in south-east Asia.

He didn't need to look up to know that Emily had walked into the lobby. He hadn't heard the lift ping, he hadn't heard the swish of a door drawing back, yet he knew. By the way the tiny hairs at the back of his neck leapt up. The words blurred on the page. The tapping of her heels on the marble echoed louder and louder as they came towards him. Deliberately taking his time, Luke closed the magazine, looked up, and his mouth went dry.

She was standing on the very spot where they'd kissed yesterday, wearing some kind of green wraparound dress the exact colour of her eyes. It fell to her knees and clung just about everywhere. His gaze roamed up, taking in the elegant sweep of hair that was caught up with an arrangement of feathers and tumbled in glossy waves over her shoulders, and then he continued his appraisal down over her curves to the very high sandals that made her long legs even longer.

Running a finger around the inside of the collar of a shirt that was suddenly choking him, Luke got to his feet. Her scent threaded towards him, and he was gripped by a lust so strong that he had to jam his hands in his pockets to stop himself from throwing her over his shoulder, bundling her back into that lift and locking them both in her room for the rest of the weekend.

'You look beautiful,' he managed hoarsely, giving her a tense smile and then clearing his throat.

Emily returned his smile with a sunnier one of her own and he was struck by a deep sense of foreboding. Telling him to get out of here now. Head straight back to Monte Carlo as fast as Pierre could get him there.

'Thank you,' said Emily, giddy with relief that he'd turned up to meet her and buzzing at his compliment. 'So do you.'

Luke Harrison dressed for a wedding was devastating. The fact that he looked tired and drawn did nothing to detract from his dark good looks, and did nothing to diminish the effect he was having on her pulse.

But, although he was staring at her as if he wanted to devour her, he didn't offer her a kiss on the cheek and she suddenly felt uncharacteristically awkward. He had an edge about him today that made her feel as if she could be walking on eggshells, and she couldn't bring herself to ask him what the 'Oh dear' had meant. If she did, it would stir up memories of that kiss, and Luke didn't look as if he was in the mood to discuss it. Much better to pretend it had never happened.

'Would you like a drink before we go?'

God, no, thought Emily. Who knew how long it would be before she stepped too heavily on those eggshells? Two hours in a confined space with him would be bad enough as it was. Why prolong the agony? 'Would you mind if we just went straight there?'

'Not at all.' Luke put a hand on her elbow to lead her out to his car. His chauffeur-driven car, if the well-built man dressed in a dark uniform and cap and standing by the rear door was anything to go by. 'Give the address to Pierre and he'll put it into the navigation system.'

Emily fished the invitation out of her bag and presented it to Pierre with a flourish. *'Voilà,'* she said, smiling up at the driver, who took it with an inclination of his head and then held the door open for her. Emily swung into the car as if she never travelled any other way, while Luke stalked round to the other side and folded himself onto the back seat beside her.

The Provence countryside had been whizzing by for about an hour before Emily had finally had enough of the crackling silence. Wasn't *she* the one who was supposed to be on edge and tense? Her ex-fiancé was, after all, within a hair's breadth of marrying another woman. To add insult to injury, she was bound to bump into people who'd taken his side after the split and whom she hadn't seen or spoken to since. Yes, *she* was the one who should be trembling in trepidation. But, bizarrely, she felt fine. Amazingly calm and collected and ready to face whatever the afternoon held in store for her.

Luke, however, who should be relaxed and looking forward to spending the afternoon drinking champagne at someone else's expense, was radiating unease and sitting unnaturally still. He was staring into the distance, probably totally unaware of the quaint towns and swathes of fields zipping past.

What on earth was the matter with him? Yesterday, for the most part, he'd been charming. Today he was decidedly unsociable and it was unsettling her. To hell with the eggshells. This silence was driving her nuts and the thought of another minute of it was unbearable.

Emily swivelled round and studied his profile. 'How were your meetings?'

Luke barely blinked before replying. 'Productive.'

Hmm, not a promising start. She tried a different topic. 'Where do you stay when you're here?'

'I have offices in Monaco.'

'Handy. But that's not what I asked.'

'One of the rooms has been converted into a bedroom. It has an *en-suite* bathroom and a dressing room.'

'You sleep in your office?' Emily couldn't keep the incredulity out of her voice.

'It makes for an easy commute,' said Luke, twisting round and shooting her a humourless smile.

'You have a chauffeur. Commuting should be a cinch.'

'He's on loan for this evening. I have a feeling I'm going to need a drink.' His face hardened and his jaw set as if in preparation for something unpleasant.

She could sympathise. 'I know what you mean.'

'I doubt it,' he said harshly.

Emily frowned. 'Don't you like weddings?'

'Not particularly.'

'Not even the church part?'

'Especially not the church part,' he said, with a vehemence that made Emily flinch.

'Why not?'

'I just don't.'

Which was one way of saying mind your own business, she supposed. 'When was the last time you were in a church?'

'Three years ago.'

'That's a long time.'

'Too long.' His voice was bleak, and she wasn't sure she wanted to know any more. Invisible barriers were springing up all around him, warning her to back off, not to pry any further.

So she sat back and contemplated what might cause such a strong dislike of churches and weddings. According to one of her girlfriends, the mere mention of either had a tendency to cause most men to break into a sweat. It certainly had with Tom, even after he'd proposed. Although he'd managed to get over that particular fear with unflattering speed.

Perhaps Luke Harrison was a commitment phobe. That might explain why he was still single when he was handsome, wealthy and intelligent.

'How on earth did you slip through the net?' she murmured, and then gasped in horror when she realised she'd said the words aloud.

'What net?'

There was no way she could pretend she didn't understand what he was talking about. Not when his eyes had narrowed and were trained on her face.

Emily gulped nervously. 'The marriage net. I'd have thought someone would have snapped you up years ago.' Why, oh, why hadn't she kept quiet? Eggshells were beginning to shatter all over the place.

A muscle started ticking in his jaw. 'Marriage isn't for me,' he bit out.

Something about his stillness, the flash of desolation in his eyes, made Emily yearn to find out why he was so against marriage. But she'd already gone way too far.

Desperately seeking to lighten the atmosphere, she gave him what she hoped was a conspiratorial smile. 'I agree. Commitment, responsibility, a relationship…' She shuddered. 'I can't think of anything worse.'

After several minutes of more thundering silence Luke rubbed a hand over his face, and when he looked at her again something seemed to have shifted inside him. The tension ebbed from his frame and his eyes cleared. 'Talking of commitment, you'd better fill me in on this wedding we're going to.'

Emily swallowed and looked out of the window. 'I know the groom. Tom's a—er…a friend of mine.' Quite why she was reluctant to reveal the nature of their relationship to Luke was a mystery. He'd find out soon enough. With any luck after she'd had a glass or two of champagne.

'Why didn't you want to go?'

'Oh, well, I—er—haven't seen him for a while. There didn't seem much point.'

'Why was Anna so keen for you to come?'

Emily stifled a sigh of exasperation. Couldn't he just let it

go? 'She thinks I need to get out more,' she said firmly. And
that was as much as she was willing to say on the matter.

Luke acknowledged her determination to change the subject
with a tiny nod. 'Who's he marrying?'

'A woman called Marianne du Champs,' she replied, adding
'perceptive' to the long list of his attributes. 'I believe she may
be a countess.'

She leaned towards the window as Pierre pulled the car up
opposite a huge looming church. Everywhere she looked
guests were milling around, the women dressed up to the nines
in the latest designer outfits, the men elegant in traditional
wedding attire.

'Ah, look,' said Emily, 'a nice, small, intimate wedding.'

She spied two of Tom's friends, who up until a year ago had
been her friends too. A tremor shook through her and her confidence wobbled. She brushed her palms against her dress and
fought back a sudden attack of nerves. Perhaps this was going
to be more gruelling than she'd imagined.

Luke climbed out of the car, walked round the bonnet and
opened the door for her. Emily swung her knees round, put her
hand in his, and in one fluid movement she was on her feet.

'That was beautifully done,' he said, offering her his arm.

'Thank you,' she replied, taking it. 'If you're trying to boost
my confidence, you're doing a good job.'

'Does your confidence need boosting?'

'Ask me in an hour.'

Some people would gossip about her presence at the
wedding of her ex-fiancé, and the grapevine would no doubt
tremble violently. But she'd just stepped out of a chauffeur-
driven car and was now on the arm of the sexiest, best-looking
man on the face of the earth. As they crossed the road, Emily
took a deep breath and rallied her strength.

'Are you all right?' asked Luke.

'Absolutely fine,' she said firmly. 'You?'

'Absolutely fine.' But he wasn't. The tension was back and

he was staring up at the church, his eyes icy blue and his face frozen.

'If it helps,' she murmured, 'there should be plenty of extraordinary headwear and stained glass to focus on.'

A glimmer of a smile hovered over his mouth for a second before his lips tightened. 'Do you want to wait out here or shall we go in?'

Emily glanced round and saw that they were attracting considerable attention. Or rather Luke was. But he seemed unaware of the appreciative looks being shot in his direction. She scanned the crowd to see if she could spot anyone she could say hello to, but there were no friendly faces among the guests. She doubted there'd be many inside either, but there was no going back now. 'Let's go in.'

He walked up the steps stiffly, and she had the impression that it was only sheer will-power that was moving him forwards and up and through the huge oak doors. As she followed him inside and her vision adjusted to the gloom she noticed that he'd gone alarmingly pale. His fingers tightened around hers and she realised that this wedding wasn't only going to be an ordeal for her.

But what could be the reason for Luke's unease? she wondered, taking one of the orders of service that were being held out by an usher. Was a fear of weddings a medical condition? Matrimoniphobia, perhaps? He didn't strike her as the sort of man who would tolerate a fear, yet he was clutching her hand as if his life depended on it.

He let her go so she could shuffle along an empty pew. Had he been dropped in the font as a baby? Had he too once been to the wedding of someone he'd cared about? A funeral, perhaps? The possibilities were endless, but it was hardly the sort of thing she could ask.

'I was right,' said Emily, glancing around before putting her handbag on the floor.

'About what?' muttered Luke.

'Hats and glass.' She tried to settle herself on the uncomfortable pew.

When Luke didn't answer she stole a quick peek at him. He was studying the church's architecture with an almost fierce intensity, but at least some colour had returned to his face. It was as if he'd gone into some sort of zone, she thought, running her fingers over the engraved front of the order of service. She was willing to bet that he was totally unaware of her presence. Or anyone else's, for that matter.

'Emily?' A voice behind her and a tap on her shoulder made her jump. She twisted round and found herself face to face with one of the few people who had stayed in touch when she and Tom split up.

'Felicity, how lovely to see you,' she said.

'Likewise. How are you? It's been ages.'

'Too long.'

'Isn't this fantastic?' Felicity waved a hand around to indicate the magnificence of the church. 'I don't think I've ever been to a wedding like it. I can't wait for the reception. Marianne's lovely, and doesn't Tom look great?' There was an awkward pause as Felicity's expression of delight turned to one of horror. She clapped both hands to her face. 'Oh, God, I'm sorry. Sometimes I only open my mouth to change feet.'

'Sorry about what?'

Felicity looked bewildered for a second. 'Well, you know. Banging on about the wedding. When Tom is marrying Marianne.'

Emily glanced at Luke, but he didn't appear to be listening. 'Don't worry about it,' she assured Felicity, who was staring at her with concern.

'Are you all right with it?'

'Heavens, yes.' She could feel herself going red. She'd been so wrapped up in what was going on with Luke that she had barely given Tom a second's thought. 'I'm happy for him. Truly,' she added at the sceptical look that crossed Felicity's face.

'I can well believe that,' she said, leaning forward. She nodded in Luke's direction and asked, 'Who's your friend?'

Emily caught the appreciative note in her voice and felt a stab of irritation. Whatever Luke was going through, he didn't need to be subjected to a barrage of questions by an over-flirtatious female.

A rustling behind them saved her from having to answer Felicity's question. 'Oh, look, I think the bride's arrived,' she said brightly, as the organ boomed the opening bars of the 'Bridal Chorus' and everyone stood and turned to watch the entrance of Marianne du Champs.

The organist then launched into the first hymn, and Emily took the opportunity to survey the congregation. As she'd suspected, she didn't spy many allies among the glamorous throng. Mainly she encountered expressions of surprise. One or two glimmers of sympathy, which she could have done without. And there was enough eyeing up of the man beside her to have her inching towards him in a distinctly proprietorial fashion.

She was just debating whether or not it would be a bit much to thread her arm through his when Tom's voice poured through the speakers and jerked her head back. Had they got to that part already?

For the first time since the ceremony had begun, and with a faint sense of shame, she turned her attention to what was happening in front of her. Her gaze rested on the man with whom at one point she'd been planning to spend her future. Tall, blond, good-looking and familiar, he was smiling down at the woman in white—the woman who at one time could have been her.

She waited for her heart to lurch, for a stab of pain, perhaps, or regret, but as she watched and heard him say his vows all she could think of was Luke and that kiss.

Which wasn't right, surely? Even if she was over Tom, shouldn't she be experiencing some sort of inner turmoil at seeing him standing up there at the altar about to marry another woman, instead of lusting after another man? She frowned. Perhaps her mind had sent her into denial without her knowledge.

Emily emptied her head of all thoughts and forced herself to focus on Tom. He was looking proud, happy and relaxed. Unlike Luke. Oh, no. How could she examine her emotions for turmoil if Luke clouded the issue? She blinked and pushed him to one side.

Now, where was she? Oh, yes. Tom. He was sliding a ring onto Marianne's finger and staring down at her with an awed expression on his face. Hang on, she thought with a frown. Did her heart just ping? And was that another one? Yes, it was definitely pinging. Thank God for that. Two tugs on her heartstrings was perfect. Just enough to reassure herself that she cared, not enough to cause her pain. What a relief. Now she could dally with Luke without any nasty insecurities popping up at inconvenient times.

And she did want to dally with him. Very much. She looked up at him. He was glowering at a window and a muscle was ticking in his jaw. Desire mingled with curiosity. Whatever the reason for Luke's phobia of churches, it clearly went a great deal deeper than a simple fear of commitment.

Luke barely heard the music and words echoing through the church, and he wasn't concentrating on the stained glass. No. He was far too busy gritting his teeth and fighting for control of his mind.

It had been three years since Grace's funeral. Three years since he'd last stepped inside a church. Of all the things that should be going through his head, skin-prickling awareness of the woman beside him was not one of them.

Yet every time they stood or sat a fresh wave of her intoxicating scent hit his perplexed brain. The memory of her in his arms, her mouth and body moving against his, rolled back into his head and he had to clench his fists to stop himself from reaching for her.

Luke sat down and studied the painting above the altar. Exhaustion. That was it. That was why his mind hadn't been working properly in the meeting yesterday and wasn't working properly now. That was why his attraction to Emily was hitting him quite so hard. He should take a break—ease up on his insane workload before he burned out. And maybe he should indulge in the 'fun' that Jack kept banging on about.

Luke heard the rustle of people standing and automatically got to his feet. He had the feeling Emily could be a lot of fun. Emily was warm and vibrant and attracted to him. Her response to his kiss had been hotter than he could have imagined.

Her arm brushed against his, making him jump as if he'd been poked with a cattle prod. That was it. He'd had enough of only half existing. It was about time he had some fun. He tore his gaze from the cherub he'd been focusing on and turned his head to look down at her. At the same time she looked up. Their gazes collided, and the leap of desire he saw in Emily's eyes decimated any remnant of doubt he might have had.

Emily nearly collapsed back down on the pew from the scorching heat of Luke's gaze, but she couldn't drag her eyes away. Her heart raced. If she combusted on the spot would it be hailed as a miracle? Her head went fuzzy. A flash of white cut across her vision. Didn't some people see a bright light before passing out? She had to get out of there before she found out.

How much longer would this blasted service go on for? Summoning every ounce of strength she possessed, she wrenched her eyes away from Luke's. And blinked in astonishment. Everyone was moving. The ceremony was over? Already? That look must have frozen them in time. And that flash of white must have been the new Mrs Thomas Green gliding back down the aisle. Nice to know Luke didn't, after all, have the power to send her into a swoon.

But the dramatic change in his demeanour was odd. From tense and edgy to carnal and predatory. It wasn't normal. Before she could analyse this any further, Luke took her arm,

clamped her against him, and starting pushing them through
the crush of people in the aisle.

'Would you like to go in the car, or shall we walk?' he
asked when they finally managed to get out of the church.

'Let's walk,' she replied. 'It's not far, and I love the smell
of Provence in summer.'

Luke's gaze slid down her body. 'Will you be able to walk
in those shoes?'

'Nope. But I won't have to.' She pulled a pair of sparkly flats
out of her bag.

'Practical,' said Luke, sliding a pair of sunglasses onto his
nose.

'Not a fan of blisters,' she said with a rueful smile. 'Can I
borrow you?'

Without waiting for an answer, she grabbed his arm and
quickly switched shoes. When she was back on her feet,
sandals dangling from one hand, there was no reason for her
other hand to still be on his arm. But for some strange reason
she was reluctant to let him go. He was so warm and hard under
her fingers, and she had to force herself to break the contact
before her hand started doing something inappropriate—like
creeping up his arm to his shoulder, to see if his muscles were
as defined as she remembered.

Reluctantly she dropped her hand and lifted her face to
smile her thanks. Without the added height of her heels, Luke
towered over her. Now that she thought about it, yesterday
she'd been wearing three-inch wedges and earlier today the
sandals. She hadn't realised quite how tall and broad he really
was. It made her feel dainty and feminine—which, at a gener-
ously proportioned five foot seven, didn't happen often.

'Let me take your shoes,' he offered.

She was hit by an image of those big hands holding her
delicate shoes, and maybe offering to put them back on when
they arrived at the château, his fingers circling her ankle,
trailing up over her calf… She swallowed and blinked rapidly.
'They wouldn't suit you.'

A hint of a smile curved his mouth and he took her shoes gently from her. 'Ready?'

'Lead on.'

She brushed down her skirt and checked herself for dust, and then looked up to find him watching her, his expression dark and serious, the sunglasses lending him a sinister air. 'What?' she asked, her heart thumping. 'Is something wrong?'

'Very wrong.' His voice had softened, deepened, and it slithered over her like silk.

'Do I have lavender in my hair?' Her hands flew up to check. 'Fluff on my dress?'

He gave his head a quick shake, hooked a finger under the bridge of his sunglasses to slide them off and took a slow step towards her.

Emily's mouth dried at the look in his eye.

'It's occurred to me that I've been somewhat remiss,' he said.

'You have?' she said, her voice suddenly hoarse.

'Mmm-hmm. I forgot to kiss you hello earlier. That wasn't very gallant.'

'It wasn't,' she agreed breathlessly, backing up against the tree and lifting her chin.

'But fortunately easily remedied.' Luke placed his hands either side of her head and leisurely scanned her face, as if deciding where to begin.

Emily's heart raced and she began to fizz with anticipation. His head came down, blotting out the sun. Her mouth tingled. But at the last minute he turned his head a fraction and his lips brushed her cheek. He stopped and drew back an inch, leaving her screaming inside with frustration.

'Now *that* wasn't very gallant,' she murmured, her eyes fixed on his mouth.

'I haven't finished yet.'

His hand found the curve of her neck and he pulled it forward so that her head tipped back and her lips parted. As his mouth closed over hers and he started to kiss her properly

Emily's head swam. Hot excitement darted through her and pooled deep inside her. She was melting…

He broke away, breathing hard. 'Better?' His eyes glittered down at her, his pupils so dilated that she could hardly see any blue.

'I'm not sure,' she said hazily, her mouth still on fire. 'I might need another demonstration just to double-check.'

'If we stay here any longer we might not get to the reception at all.'

'Fine by me,' murmured Emily. As far as she was concerned she could stay pinned up against that tree kissing Luke for ever.

'What about Anna and her spies?'

Emily felt as if a bucket of cold water had been thrown over her. Summoning strength into her watery limbs, she pushed herself off the tree and checked that her feathers were still in place. 'You're right,' she said, stifling a sigh and joining him in a stroll along the avenue.

As the magnificent château standing at the far end of the road came into focus Emily's breath caught. Duck-egg-blue shutters framed three storeys of windows set in weathered grey stone. Golden light spilled out of the windows, casting a fairytale-like glow over the darkening evening. Elegant cypress trees surrounded the house, allowing only a tantalising glimpse of the grounds.

They followed a stream of guests through an arch in a wall that led down onto a wide balcony overlooking immaculate formal gardens. Torches blazed along the gravel paths. The fountain in the centre gushed, droplets of water twinkling in the firelight like diamonds. The effect was magical.

'You see,' said Emily, sweeping an arm around to encompass all she saw. 'This is the sort of place a knight should have.'

'I'll bear it in mind,' said Luke dryly, his eyes scanning the throng. 'There's no pleasing some people. I thought I'd gone above and beyond the call of duty with the shoe thing.'

'You did. It was unexpected and very noble.'

'And I did rectify the remiss kiss,' he pointed out.

Emily laughed and gave an apologetic shrug. 'What can I say? I'm a demanding damsel.'

'Would the demanding damsel like a drink?'

'She certainly would.'

He ran a finger down her cheek. 'I'll be back in a second. Don't go anywhere.'

With Luke weaving his way through the crowds towards a waiter bearing a tray laden with bubbling glasses, and Tom heading purposefully towards her, Emily realised she couldn't move even if she'd wanted to.

CHAPTER FOUR

'EMILY.'

Emily dragged her gaze from Luke's back and her heart flip-flopped as she stared up at her ex-fiancé. Into the face she'd once thought would be the first thing she looked at in the morning and the last thing she saw at night. A face that she hadn't seen for a year, but she still remembered every contour of it. A lock of fair hair had fallen over his forehead, and she had to clench her fists to prevent her hand from automatically reaching out and pushing it back. That right belonged to someone else now.

Tom was looking at her as if he wasn't sure whether to kiss her on the cheek or not, and her heart twinged. To spare him any further awkwardness, she reached up and gave him a quick peck instead. Her eyes closed for a second and she inhaled, expecting to feel the warm familiar smell of him waft through her and steeling herself to deal with it. But instead of familiar he smelled weird. Spicy, woody, musky. Different.

'Tom,' she said, drawing back and blinking to hide her confusion.

'It's good to see you, Em. Thank you for coming.' He shifted his weight from one foot to the other. 'I wasn't sure you would.'

'Oh, well—you know,' she said with a shrug. 'I was at a loose end this weekend.'

He smiled and his shoulders relaxed. 'You look well.'

'I am well,' she replied. 'Thank you for inviting me. Congratulations. Marianne seems lovely.'

'She is.' The pride in his voice was unmistakable.

There was a brief silence. Emily watched as Tom's eyes flickered everywhere but at her, and marvelled at how relaxed she felt now that she was actually seeing him again and in these circumstances. Yes, her heart had hurt a little earlier, and still felt a bit on the tender side, but every twinge lessened in intensity. The past year, with her sister providing a shoulder to cry on and a steady stream of white wine, had obviously healed more of her wounds than she'd realised.

Now, thinking about it, all she felt for him was a sort of fond nostalgia. Nostalgia that was rapidly turning to impatience. Surely he had *something* to say to her? They'd been together for five years, for heaven's sake. At the very least he owed her some sort of effort at small talk. Had he always been so useless at making conversation?

When the silence became excruciating Emily couldn't bear it any longer. 'It was a beautiful service,' she said. 'Sublime flowers.'

'Yes, they're all from the estate.'

'It's a magnificent house. Will you be living here?'

'Nearby.'

'How lovely.'

Five years of going out, and this was what they were reduced to? A handful of awkward platitudes? Emily inwardly sighed. Tom had done the polite thing. They'd navigated successfully through the most delicate of situations, and he'd done his duty, so what was he doing still here? 'I'm sure you must have lots of other people to greet, Tom. Please do go ahead.'

He shifted again and his eyes slid from hers. 'I just wanted to say I'm sorry for the way things turned out between us.'

Emily's heart skipped a beat. Surely he wasn't going to rake all over this again? On his wedding day?

'Honestly, Tom, it's fine. It was for the best. We wanted dif-

ferent things. You know that, I know that. We've both moved
on. Haven't we?'

Emily heard a steely edge creep into her voice and watched
him straighten.

'I guess we have. Who's the chap you've brought along?
New boyfriend?'

'My plus one,' she said. An image of Luke flashed into her
head and Emily found herself assessing Tom's features critically. Was there a hint of fleshiness at his jawline? The begin-
nings of a receding hairline? Her eyes flickered over his tall
frame. Had he been indulging in a little too much fine French
food?

Wishing that Luke would hurry up with that drink, Emily
decided she'd wasted quite enough time on Tom. Somewhere
in the throng was a god of a man whose kisses promised a
heaven she'd quite like to explore.

'I really ought to go and find him,' she said, looking around
until she spied Luke a few feet away, a glass in each hand,
talking to someone obscured by a towering flower arrangement. Who was it? Who had made him laugh like that? Emily
used the excuse of a guest bumping into her to slide across
enough to see Felicity curling a hand on Luke's arm and
reaching up to whisper in his ear.

'Wait, Em. Before you do, there's something I need to tell
you.'

'Hmm?' she murmured, stifling the urge to race over to the
pair of them, grab one of the glasses Luke was holding and hurl
it down Felicity's cleavage.

'Marianne's pregnant.'

Emily's attention whipped back to Tom. Her vision blurred
for a second. 'Congratulations again,' she said, her voice
sounding steady but distant. It was, after all, what Tom had
always wanted.

No, she amended tartly, not always. When they'd first
started going out they'd been in perfect agreement about not
having children. But shortly after they'd got engaged Tom had

revealed that he did in fact want a family, and had done for quite some time. He'd thought he'd be able to change her mind, especially after proposing. Emily, shell-shocked first by the revelation and then by the realisation that the person who should have known her best of all had assumed her position on the subject was negotiable, had felt betrayed. She knew that some people might consider her decision unnatural, but she had her reasons and she'd always thought she'd had an ally in Tom. But apparently not. In the end the unexpected deadlock had meant the end of their relationship.

'I didn't want you to hear it from anyone else.'

'I appreciate it.' She gave him a brittle smile. 'Thank you for telling me. Now, go and circulate. Find your wife.'

'Thanks, Em,' said Tom. 'Enjoy the party.' He dropped a kiss on her cheek and gave her arm a quick squeeze before moving off to shake the hand of another guest.

'So, Luke, how did you meet Emily?'

Luke was struggling to pay attention to Felicity. Ever since she'd cornered him on his way back to Emily he'd only really been half listening to her anyway. He'd laughed at what he'd imagined were the appropriate times, and responded to her chatter automatically, while wondering how he could extricate himself from the hand on his arm without seeming too offensive.

'A mutual friend,' he muttered, glancing over at Emily. He was finding it hard to concentrate on anything other than a long-forgotten urge drumming through him to have her hot and naked and beneath him. Which was why he'd kept one eye on Emily's exchange with the groom. He hadn't liked what he'd seen. Whatever the details of their relationship, Tom was without doubt more than merely a work colleague.

Luke had watched the expressions flit across her face as they spoke. Bewilderment, regret, maybe, detachment, a flash of impatience, and then something that had made his jaw clench. The sparkle faltered in the depths of her eyes and the colour drained from her face.

His eyes narrowed as he realised that he wasn't the only one who was interested in what was happening between Emily and Tom.

'I ought to deliver this,' said Luke abruptly, indicating the glass in his left hand, vaguely aware that he'd interrupted Felicity's stream of chatter.

'She must be needing it,' said Felicity. 'Poor girl.'

The pitying tone of Felicity's voice as much as her words snagged his attention quicker than any amount of eyelash-fluttering and coy smiles had. 'Oh, really? Why's that?'

Felicity leaned forward conspiratorially. 'Well, it can't be easy for her. I mean, the *humiliation*. She's so brave.'

He raised an eyebrow calculated to encourage Felicity to gossip as she so clearly wanted to do.

'Tom and Emily used to be engaged.'

Luke went still. 'I didn't know that,' he murmured, his brain rapidly processing the information. No wonder she hadn't wanted to attend the wedding.

'No one really knows why they split. I think it was because Tom's mother is a crashing snob and never thought Emily was good enough for her only son. Others say it's because Emily has a fear of commitment and responsibility.'

Luke's brows snapped together as he watched Tom leave Emily alone in the crowd and oblivious to the sidelong glances and whispers. She needed an ally and a drink. He muttered an apology to Felicity and made his way to where Emily was standing frozen to the spot.

'Are you all right?' he asked, putting the glass in her hand.

'Couldn't be better,' she said, with a brightness that sounded strained.

'Good,' he said. He planted a hard swift kiss on her mouth. 'That should give people something else to talk about,' he murmured, noting with some satisfaction that her eyes were sparkling again and her cheeks had more colour.

He wound an arm around her waist and directed her towards a gate he'd spied in the wall. He pushed it open and led her down the steps into a sunken patio. Light filtered through the entrance, illuminating the path but leaving the rest of the patio in shadow. Honeysuckle tumbled down the walls, permeating the warm air with a sweet, heady fragrance.

'Why did you bring me down here?' asked Emily, her gaze sweeping over the patio.

'So we can have this conversation in private.'

'What conversation?'

'The one where you tell me why you didn't happen to mention that you were once engaged to the groom.'

'Ah, that one.'

'Yes, that one.'

'How did you find out?'

'Your friend Felicity.'

The way Emily was studiously not looking at him was beginning to irritate him, so he put his fingers under her chin and gently turned her head, lifting her face until she had no option *but* to look at him. 'So?' he asked softly, when it became obvious that she was stalling.

'Does it really matter?'

'You tell me.'

Emily let out a little sigh and he saw the tension drain from her body. He dropped his hand before it could curve round the back of her neck and pull her to him.

'I guess that's only fair, seeing as I did drag you all the way out here.' She took a sip of champagne. 'I went out with Tom for five years, lived with him for the last two, got engaged to him and then disengaged.'

'What happened?'

She chewed on her lip and her gaze slid to the lion's head spouting water from the wall. 'Nothing spectacular.' She shrugged. 'We simply drifted apart.'

Just like that? thought Luke sceptically as she set her glass down on the stone bench. Five years condensed into a dozen or so words? The flatness of her tone almost disguised the hurt and pain, but not quite, and Luke felt his stomach clench. His head went fuzzy for a second and he had to shake it to clear it. He blinked and focused back on the woman standing in front of him, staring at him with mesmerising green eyes. His mouth went dry and he cleared his throat. 'Not just a work colleague, then?'

'Oh, well, yes—in the beginning. That's how we met. I was temping at the company where he worked. IT consulting. Very tedious.' She stuck up her chin. 'I'm sure you don't really want to know all the gory details.'

He did. For some unfathomable reason he did. 'Not particularly.' His fingers tightened around the champagne flute and he downed what was left in the glass.

'If he hadn't ended it,' Emily was saying, her jaw set and a glint in her eye, 'I would have. I'm totally over it. I didn't need to come here to know that, but Anna had this idea that if I didn't come people would think I was so prostrate with grief that I was unable to lever myself out of bed.'

'Do you care what people think?'

'Not in the slightest.' She gave him a small mischievous smile. 'But I must admit I was a bit curious.'

'Why didn't you say anything?'

Emily stared at him as if he was mad. 'Hmm, let me see. Telling a complete stranger that my ex-fiancé's invited me to his wedding to the woman he left me for. Doesn't exactly do much for a girl's image, does it? And then rashly asking said complete stranger to go with me to the wedding, because the idea of going with a very good-looking man was more appealing than going alone?' She shook her head ruefully. 'Pathetic.'

She crossed her arms over her chest. Luke's gaze dropped to the deepening V of her cleavage and a bolt of desire shot straight down to his groin.

'If it's any consolation,' he said hoarsely, 'I think the man's a fool.'

'Thank you.'

Luke couldn't resist any longer. He wrapped his arms around her and lowered his mouth to hers. He felt her melt against him, and as they kissed a tremor ran through him. The glass slipped from his fingers and shattered on the stone, making them both jump.

'Oops,' she said shakily.

'I'll buy them a dozen more as a wedding present.'

He drew back, breathing hard, and stared down into her eyes, glazed with desire, her lips wet and parted.

'What was that for?' she said huskily, drawing back to unfold her arms.

'I'm finding it increasingly hard to keep my hands off you.'

'Oh,' she murmured, sliding her hands up over his chest. 'In that case, don't let me stop you.'

Her touch burned through the layers of clothing to scorch his skin. He traced the line of her lower lip with his thumb until her breathing became ragged and her eyelids fluttered down. The tip of her tongue darted out to touch his thumb, sending fire twisting through him. With a groan his lips met hers and the rhythmic beat of desire flared between them as their tongues tangled. What the hell was it about her that sent his temperature into the stratosphere? His brain fogged. Had someone spiked his champagne with absinthe?

Deciding to find fun with Emily was definitely one of his better ideas, he thought with satisfaction as he broke off the kiss and dragged in a shaky breath. His gaze fixed on her mouth—red, swollen, luscious—and the primal need to taste her again surged in him.

'I'm definitely over it,' muttered Emily, her eyes still closed and her voice low and breathy.

'It doesn't do much for a man's ego when the woman in his arms is picturing someone else.' Luke's mouth hovered milli-metres over hers. 'I must be losing my touch.' He could feel her heart hammering against his, although with desire or mor-tification that she'd been caught out he couldn't tell.

A sexy smile curved her mouth, and suddenly he didn't

really care. 'If you are,' she breathed against his mouth, 'I'd be very happy to help you find it.'

'So selfless.'

Emily laughed, and Luke covered her mouth with his and kissed her until her laugh turned to moans of pleasure.

She suddenly stilled in his arms. Luke jerked back and looked down at her in the flickering darkness.

'What is it now?'

Emily smiled. 'Just something I remembered. What was that "Oh, dear" all about?'

'What?'

'Yesterday afternoon,' she prompted, 'after we kissed in the lobby. You said "Oh, dear" before marching out of the hotel.'

Luke frowned. 'Did I say that out loud?'

'You did. What did you mean?'

Luke rubbed a brown hand along his jaw as the image of them locked together flashed into his head. That kiss had blown him away, hurled him off balance and nearly shattered his control. If she hadn't hesitated for that instant who knew where they'd have ended up? 'You've turned out to be rather more than I expected. When I won that auction, I didn't anticipate being quite so attracted to the lot.'

'Oh.' There was a pause as this sank in. 'But that's a good thing, right?'

He hesitated before answering, his gaze transfixed by the feathers dancing around her head in the light. 'I'm not sure.'

She let out a little indignant huff. 'How flattering.'

Luke tilted his head. Then he pulled her hips against him, so she could feel just what she was doing to him. He leaned down and murmured in her ear, 'Is that flattering enough for you?'

He felt her shiver. 'It all depends what you're going to do about it,' she murmured back, the warmth of her breath making his skin contract.

Luke went still. Was she really saying what he thought she

was saying? He drew back to check her face, and the seductive smile curving her mouth had his blood pounding along his veins.

'Well?' she said.

The demands of his body were telling him exactly what he was going to do about it. To hell with this bloody reception. 'The way I see it, we have two options. We can either stay here and provide fodder for the gossips…'

'Or?'

His pulse was racing. 'Or we can go.'

Her eyes darkened. 'Go where?'

'Somewhere we can continue this in private. Which is it to be?'

A tremble shuddered though her. He saw it, and had to hold himself back from making the decision for her.

'Stay or go?' he said, the desire throbbing inside him making him sound harsh.

'Go.'

'Sure?'

'Never more so.'

Luke grabbed her hand and practically dragged her back through the guests, who were drifting towards the colonnaded courtyard where dinner was taking place.

'Shouldn't we say goodbye? Or at least apologise for missing dinner?' she said breathlessly.

'We should,' he said, without breaking his stride.

Emily's pace quickened and her fingers wound more tightly round his. 'I'll write a letter.'

Emily jammed herself into the corner of the car, pressing herself into the leather. They were halfway back to the hotel and the atmosphere inside the car was electric with desire. Luke's kisses on the patio had obliterated everything except the need to have his hands and mouth roaming all over her. Her body was trembling, overwhelmed with such longing that she was incapable of thought. She glanced over at Luke, who was staring at her with eyes that were navy. His face was tight. A muscle ticked in his jaw.

'Come here,' he said.

'No,' she breathed. One touch and she'd lose control. She'd be on his lap, purring into his ear and pulling his clothes off, and probably frightening the life out of Pierre.

'Then I'll just have to come over to you.'

'Why?' She clutched the door handle, trying to make herself smaller.

'Because I want to tell you all the things I'm going to do to you and I don't want Pierre to hear.'

Emily shook her head. Her pulse raced. The dragging magnetism was getting harder and harder to resist. 'It's all right. I can imagine,' she said weakly.

Luke's eyes gleamed. 'I don't think you can possibly imagine the plans I have for those feathers.'

Her heart jumped and her skin prickled. 'What sort of plans?' Her voice was hoarse.

'Unwind yourself and I'll tell you.' He unknotted his tie and pulled it off. Emily watched the red silk slowly slither around his neck, teasing her, taunting her—the beginning of something they'd have to wait hours to complete.

Helpless to resist, she let go of the door handle, uncrossed her legs and slid over the leather until their thighs touched from hip to knee.

Luke reached his arm over the back of the seat, taking her hand in his as he bent his head towards her ear and started to tell her exactly what he was intending to do with the feathers.

In the inky darkness of the car Luke's words, full of sensual promise, and the feel of his thumb stroking relentlessly over her wrist, her palm, her fingers, gradually dissolved Emily into a quivering puddle of lust. Every cell in her body hummed with a desire so strong it was almost painful. She trembled and throbbed and ached. She had to bite hard on her lip to stop whimpers pouring from her mouth.

Oh, God, thought Emily, as embarrassment filtered though

her desire. She ventured a glance at Pierre through the rearview mirror, but, like the true professional he was, his attention was fixed firmly on the road ahead. What must he be thinking?

By the time they arrived at the hotel Emily was beyond caring. At one point when Pierre had gone round a corner her hand had accidentally on purpose brushed over Luke's erection. She'd heard his sharp inhalation and so she'd done it again and again—until his fingers had snapped round her wrist and stopped her.

Now all she wanted to do was wrap herself around him and have him sink into her and satisfy this insane craving. Her heart was about to burst from her chest. Bidding a hasty goodnight to Pierre, she tumbled out of the car.

They didn't speak as they crossed the lobby towards the lift, and yet awareness crackled between them. The arrow showed that the lift was at the top floor and Emily let out a tiny groan of frustration. Luke jabbed the button and then thrust his hands into his pockets. Emily fixed her gaze on the arrow as it began to move in an agonisingly slow arc. Seconds had never felt so long. Every part of her body was tight with anticipation.

Once in the lift, Luke leaned against one side and Emily against the other, and for the interminable journey back up to her floor they just stared at each other. Emily saw naked desire in his eyes and knew that he'd see the same in hers. Then his gaze travelled over her, slowly, lazily, stripping her bare from head to toe, and her knees nearly gave way. The lift was going so damned slowly. The frustration was making her demented. *Come on, come on,* she willed, and finally, finally it pinged and the doors swept back.

'What number?' he grated.

'Two-one-six.'

Which way was it? She couldn't remember. Luke's hand gripped her arm and he propelled her in the right direction.

Emily's fingers shook as she tried to insert her card into the door. Luke took it from her and a second later they were in the room and she was in Luke's arms, his mouth slamming down on hers. She threw her arms round his neck and wound her legs round his waist. He backed her against the door, pinning her against it, not taking his mouth from hers for a second. Emily threw her handbag down and pulled off her feathers. She ran her hands over his shoulders, frantically pushing aside his jacket and waistcoat and yanking his shirt up. Hands shaking, she undid his buttons and pushed the shirt off, first down one arm and then the other, and finally her hands were on his bare flesh.

She was desperate to feel all of him and her fingers took over, sweeping up the muscles of his arms to his broad shoulders, while his mouth continued its devastating assault on her senses.

Luke broke away, eyes glittering, breathing raspy. Emily let out a groan of disappointment. 'No,' she mumbled in protest, clinging to him.

'I need to get you out of that dress.'

He stepped back, taking her with him, cupping her bottom against him as he walked her over to the bed. He dropped her onto the sheets and for a moment just stared at her. Emily caught sight of herself in the mirror. Lying knees bent, her dress rucked up around her hips, eyes glittering and mouth red and swollen. With her hair tousled round her face she looked wild and wanton, and almost pulsating with desire.

But instead of joining her, he froze, his face twisting as if he was in actual physical pain.

Her heart stopped. 'What is it?'

Luke raked a hand through his hair. 'I didn't plan this,' he said hoarsely. 'I don't have anything.'

Relief poured through her. 'Bathroom cupboard.'

She didn't have the chance to worry about the fact that protection hadn't crossed her mind. Luke was back in the blink of an eye, dropping a handful of condoms on the bedside table, kicking off his shoes and stripping off the rest of his clothes. Emily swallowed as she drank in the sight of him before he sank down onto the bed with her. He was all lean, tanned muscle, his chest sprinkled with hair that narrowed down to his erection, thick and hard and straining.

He pushed a lock of hair off her face and rubbed a thumb over her trembling lip.

And then he was undoing the ties of her dress and she was wriggling, lying back in her bra and knickers and pulling him with her.

Finally his hands were on her, sliding over the skin of her shoulders, burning a trail over her collarbone, reaching down to cup her breast though the lace of her bra. Emily moaned as sparks of desire shot through the centre of her. She arched against his hand and squirmed as his hand moved lower, tracing the outline of her knickers and down over her thigh. As his fingers trailed back up, skimming over her sex, her heart slammed in her chest.

'Shoes,' he muttered.

'No time,' she groaned, as Luke reached a hand behind her and undid her bra. Quickly dispensing with the flimsy fabric, he skimmed a hand over her breasts, her stomach, her hip. Quivering, Emily felt herself spiralling out of control. 'Don't make me wait,' she moaned against his mouth, and lifted her hips to help him as he pulled her knickers down her legs and threw them aside.

'I won't,' he rasped, and he took her nipple in his mouth. Emily nearly fainted with desire. She could feel the waves of pleasure building, such intense ripples of delight that she didn't think she could take much more.

'Please,' she whimpered.

He leaned away from her and she heard the tear of the condom packet. He swung back over her, staring down at her with such fierce intensity that she nearly came then and there. Then he was nudging her knees apart and lowering himself on his elbows. He entered her with one smooth thrust. Emily gasped as he filled her, pressing inside her, swelling, pulsating. Her hands on his back felt his muscles straining as he fought for control. He withdrew and plunged again, slamming into her over and over, until with a tiny scream she hurtled over the edge, shattering into a million pieces, gasping for air as the waves of pleasure thundered through her. Luke's mouth came down on hers, swallowing her gasps, and with a harsh groan he thrust deep inside her and followed her into blissful oblivion.

Emily woke with a lazy, satisfied smile on her face. She just knew she did. She squinted at the sliver of bright morning light that squeezed through the gap in the curtains and rubbed her eyes. What a night! Who could have imagined that a hot tub would be so much fun? Or that Luke would turn out to be quite so creative with room service? And the feathers… Well, all she could think was that Anna had been right: Luke *was* a man of his word. Every single one of them…

All sorts of muscles she'd never known she had tingled. Her body seemed to be *made* for sex. At least sex with Luke. No one else had ever given her multiple orgasms or taken her to such heights of ecstasy. And to think if she'd married Tom she'd never have known.

Luke must be exhausted. She'd woken in the middle of the night to find him standing on the balcony, staring out to sea. She'd got out of bed, wrapped herself in a towel still damp from the hot tub, and padded over to see if he was all right. He'd turned, the moonlight casting silvery shadows across his face. Emily had scoured his expression but it had been blank, reawakening desire the only sign of emotion in his eyes as they'd raked over her scantily clad form. Then he'd taken her back to bed for another bout of sex that had left her utterly shattered.

She stretched languidly and rolled over. To an empty space on the other side of the bed. Frowning, Emily listened for sounds that Luke might be in the shower or out on the balcony. But the only thing she could hear in the still silence of the early Sunday morning was the sound of her heart thumping away. She was alone.

Her skin prickled with foreboding as she sat up, clutching the sheet to her chest, and ran a hand through her hair. She looked round the room. His clothes had disappeared. Perhaps he'd gone for a swim, a workout in the gym, a run along the beach? Emily's heart lifted before sinking once more. Sure. In his morning suit? It was more likely he'd taken one look at her tangled mess of hair, smudged eye make-up and less-than-perfect figure and done a runner.

Her heart drooped and she flopped back onto the pillows. Whichever way she looked at it, it wasn't good. An image of his shocked expression when he'd agreed to take her to the wedding flashed into her head. He hadn't wanted to go in the first place. That much had been obvious.

And then look at the way she'd behaved. Leaping into bed with him, practically begging him to ravish her having only just met him. She clapped a hand over her eyes. Oh, he might have been equally keen, but there were different rules for men, weren't there? In the cold light of day he might well have decided she was a complete tart and regretted the whole thing.

She was still lying there half an hour later, struggling to justify his absence against the fairly compelling evidence that she'd been abandoned, when the phone rang. Emily jumped and scooted over to the phone, nearly falling out of bed in the process.

'Hello?' she said, snatching up the receiver.

'It's Luke.'

Emily's heart quickened at the sound of his voice. The same voice that only hours ago had told her how incredible she was and how amazing she felt. She shivered. Maybe he was ringing to find out what she wanted for breakfast. Oh, for goodness' sake. How many more straws could she clutch at? A more key question was how was she going to play this? She bit her lip. Breezy. That would be good. Breezy and relaxed. Not clingy and desperate. She was definitely not going to ask where he was and what he was doing.

'Good morning,' she said, perfectly breezily. 'Um, where are you?' Oops.

'I'm at the office.'

The office? On a Sunday morning? He must have been desperate to get away. 'What are you doing there?'

'There's a crisis on the Dubai markets. I'm sorry.'

She shut her eyes tight. Even the most over-active imagination wouldn't have dreamed up that excuse. And it *was* an excuse, wasn't it? Because had she heard his mobile ring? No. The beep of a text? No. The whine of a television? No. So how had he *known* about a so-called crisis in Dubai? 'Oh, right.'

'I didn't want to wake you.'

'Sure.' If there was a crisis, wouldn't people be shouting in the background, frantically buying and selling and generally panicking?

'I'm not sure when I'll be finished here. The plane's available all day, so why don't you have a lie-in or hit the beach, and I'll come and find you when I'm done.'

'I may just do that.' To her ears her voice sounded brittle, a little too bright.

There was a heavy silence. 'Look, Emily, I have to go. But we'll talk later.' He sounded as if his attention was on other things—as if the phone call he'd made to her was an irritation he could do without. Something snapped inside her. Dignity was pretty much the only thing she could cling to at that moment. Dignity and the bedsheet.

'Don't worry about it,' she said, injecting her voice with a breezy lack of concern she didn't feel. 'Thank you, Luke, for ferrying me to France and accompanying me to the wedding and…er…things. It was fun. I hope your crisis sorts itself out. Goodbye.'

Without waiting for him to answer, and fearing that she might not be able to disguise the disappointment in her voice, she replaced the receiver gently in the cradle.

Sighing deeply, she got up and went into the bathroom. She stared at herself in the mirror—at the messy hair, smudged mascara and flushed cheeks—an image which was worse than she could have envisaged. She smiled ruefully at her reflection. *Well, Emily, it looks like you've just had your first one-night stand.*

CHAPTER FIVE

LUKE slammed the ball against the wall and took grim pleasure from the stinging in his muscles from the force with which he'd hit it.

Jack lunged and ducked, shoes thudding and squeaking on the floor of the squash court as he removed himself from the path of the ball whizzing towards him. Breathing heavily, he bent over with his hands on his knees. 'Right. That's enough,' he said. 'I concede.'

'We're in the middle of a game,' said Luke.

Jack straightened. 'Yeah, well, I'd quite like to come out of it alive, and the way you're playing I'm not sure that's going to happen. So, if you don't mind, I'll quit while I'm still more or less standing.'

Luke frowned and lifted his arm to wipe his brow with the towelling band on his wrist. 'You're out of shape.'

'Nope. You're out of control.'

'I'm never out of control.'

'That's the trouble. Tell you what,' said Jack, slapping him on the back and slinging his towel round his neck, 'buy me a beer, tell me what's put you in this mood, and I'll let it slide.'

Twenty minutes later Luke set a pint of beer on the table in front of Jack. He probably owed him more than that, he thought grudgingly. It wasn't the first time he'd thrashed his frustration out during a squash game. It was one of the reasons he enjoyed playing against Jack, who could usually give as good as he got, sometimes even better. He hadn't meant to annihilate Jack out there on the squash court. He hadn't even realised he'd been playing with such ferocity. No point in wondering what had caused it. He knew full well. And he wasn't about to divulge it to anyone—least of all Jack.

'So what's up?' said Jack, taking a long slurp of beer and sighing in appreciation.

Luke shrugged. 'The usual. Stress.'

'Work?'

'What else?'

Jack raised his eyebrows. 'You need to let up. By the way, how was Nice?'

Now, there was a question. Luke's mind whipped back to Saturday night. It didn't take much effort. The long, hot night had been replaying in his head in Technicolor with surround sound. The incredible way Emily had exploded in his arms again and again, the feel of her convulsing around him, her smooth satiny skin and her warm, wet mouth creating devastation on his body.

And then the way she'd upped and left.

'Busy.'

'What was she like?'

Hot, amazing, mind-blowingly sexy… Luke shifted as his jeans tightened uncomfortably.

'What was who like?'

'The green-bikinied damsel in distress. Was she as desperate as I thought?'

Luke clamped down on the urge to thump the smile off Jack's face. He sat back, adopted a bored expression and studied his beer. 'She was fine.'

Jack's jaw dropped. '*Fine*? That's all? I should have known you wouldn't take advantage of such a God-given opportunity. You never have with any of the women I've introduced you to.' He shook his head in despair. 'I should never have let you win.'

A red mist descended into Luke's head at the thought of

Jack laying a finger on Emily. He might be his best friend, but Jack's reputation was devilish.

However, his observation was startlingly accurate. Luke *hadn't* ever been tempted by any of the women Jack had thrown in his path. And some of them had been stunning. More beautiful than Emily. So what was it about her that had him prowling around in alternating states of arousal and irritation? The image of Emily writhing in his arms, smiling seductively, had been burning in his head ever since he'd gone back to the hotel and found she'd already left. He'd tried to ignore it for days, but it was not going away.

'What did you expect me to do, Jack?' he said blandly.

'Have a bit of fun.'

'Like you, you mean?'

'And like you used to.'

'Not any more.'

'You could do worse. Losing yourself in the arms of a beautiful woman is better than killing a friend on a squash court.'

Luke let out a hollow laugh. How ironic. Jack thought sex would relieve his stress, when it was sex that was causing it in the first place.

'She wasn't my type,' he muttered. In the past, when he'd been single and out with Jack, he'd always gone for brunettes. Which was another reason for wondering what Emily's appeal was. Perhaps he was further along the road to burnout than he'd originally thought.

'It doesn't have to be for ever, Luke,' said Jack. 'You don't have to marry any of them.'

'Thanks for the advice,' said Luke tightly, deciding that the conversation was well and truly over. 'On a different note,' he said, 'what's the name of the temping agency you use?'

'No idea, but I can find out if you like. What do you need doing?'

'Just some bits and pieces round the office.'

'What's wrong with the agency you use?'

'Going downhill.' Much like his integrity.

* * *

Emily toyed with her wine glass. She'd been feeling strange ever since she'd got back from France. Edgy, restless, unsettled. Much as she tried—and she'd tried extremely hard over the past week—she couldn't stop remembering the night with Luke. When she'd first got back to London she'd secretly hoped he'd get in touch, but as the days passed the likelihood of him picking up the phone became more and more remote. Her head had reluctantly come to terms with it. Her body, on the other hand, was slow in catching up.

Daytime wasn't a problem. She'd spent the week temping at an advertising agency and the work had been fun and stimulating. But the nights… The nights were terrible. In the dark solitude of her bedroom the memories descended and any hope of sleep vanished. As a result, she was walking around like a zombie.

'So you left?' said Anna.

Emily rubbed her eyes and nodded. 'What else could I do? I was hardly going to wait around for Luke like some desperate clingy female. He might never have shown up.'

Anna pursed her lips thoughtfully. 'I suppose the Dubai emergency could have been genuine.'

Emily shrugged. 'Possibly. Hard to check when you don't know what sort of emergency.'

She heard the front door slam and the thud of a briefcase in the hall. She saw a smile light up her sister's face and experienced a brief pang of envy. What was it like to feel that way about someone? She'd certainly never felt like that about Tom, except maybe in the beginning. But Anna and David had been married for four years and they were still mad about each other.

She watched her brother-in-law drop a light kiss on his wife's mouth and smile into her eyes, and she realised that it was only her presence that was stopping him from hauling Anna to her feet and kissing her more fiercely.

Something stabbed at her heart. Loneliness? No, that was ridiculous. She was the least lonely person she knew. She had

an extremely full life. Lots of friends, great jobs… She fixed
a smile to her face as David bent to kiss her cheek.

'Hello, Em,' he said, straightening and surveying the scene.
He nodded thoughtfully and rubbed his jaw. 'Hmm, a Monday
evening, two women—sisters at that—and a bottle of wine. Do
you mind if I retreat?'

Anna nodded. 'Good idea, darling. You may not want to
hear us ripping Luke Harrison to shreds.'

David stopped in the doorway. 'Luke Harrison?'

'Yes.'

'What's he done to deserve dismemberment?'

'Never mind that,' said Anna, eyeing her husband closely.
'Do you know him?'

David looked at them warily. 'Only by reputation.'

Anna rose and pulled her husband back to the table. 'Just a
few details, darling,' she said sweetly, 'and then you can
retreat.'

Emily smiled at the panic that flitted across David's face and
hoped that her burning curiosity wasn't too obvious. 'What do
you know about him?' she said casually.

'He's some kind of genius. Very successful, very shrewd,
very driven, very competitive. Private. And apparently a workaholic.' Tell me something I don't already know, Emily thought
as David paused. 'Actually, it's a coincidence you mentioning
him…' he said, frowning.

Emily felt a trickle of trepidation run down her spine.
'Why's that?' she asked, not at all sure she wanted to hear.

'There's a strange rumour whipping round the City.'

'There always is,' said Anna.

'Something about an internet auction. A bet with a friend
over some girl. I heard Luke won. Crazy money, apparently,'
he added, pouring himself a glass of wine. 'Anyway, why are
you interested in him?'

Emily's blood ran cold and her head spun. A bet? A *bet*?
What sort of a bet? 'I'm not the slightest bit interested in him,'

she said, reaching for the bottle with a trembling hand. 'Luke who?'

David looked bemused. 'I'm afraid you've lost me.'

'Female logic, darling,' said Anna, standing up and ushering her husband out of the room. 'You wouldn't understand.'

So much for all that rubbish about being curious, wanting adventure and having meetings in Monte Carlo anyway. She'd thought that had sounded flaky at the time. A bet was much more likely for a couple of testosterone-driven playboys. She could see it now. Two men, too many beers, an irresistible challenge. Just how far had it gone? *Hey, I bet you can't get this girl into bed. I bet I can.* Was that why Luke had accompanied her to the church, despite his obvious reluctance? All those smouldering kisses and steamy looks? Had it really been nothing more than determination to win a bet? Had he had to produce *evidence*?

Oh, God. If she let it, her imagination would run wild. She dismissed the voice in her head that was saying Luke wasn't like that, wouldn't do something like that. Look at the way Tom had behaved. And how well had she really known Luke, after all?

Anna came back into the kitchen, extracted the bottle from Emily's fingers and filled her glass. 'I'm sorry, darling.'

Emily stuck her chin in her hand and shrugged. 'Doesn't matter. Luke and this so-called friend of his are obviously jerks of the highest order. I shall just move on. Isn't that what you're always telling me to do?'

'Yes, but…' Anna trailed off, anguish twisting her features.

'But nothing.' Emily forced herself to give her sister a brave smile. 'A one-night stand is hardly something to fuss about. I'll get over it. In fact, you know something? I think I already have.'

A shrill ring tone shattered the silence. For one insane moment Emily imagined it was Luke, calling to see how she was. It happened every time her phone rang and she was sick of it.

'Hang on,' she said, instructing her heart to resume normal behaviour as she rummaged around in her bag for her mobile. If she banged her head on the solid wood table, would it knock some sense into her? 'Hello?'

'Emily? It's Sarah.'

See? she told herself. Not Luke. Sarah. Her manager.

'Listen, I know you wanted this week off, but I've got a last-minute urgent need for a temp. Great money and good hours. It's only for the remainder of the week. Apparently the girl they had today was worse than useless. Say you'll do it. Pretty please?'

Emily sighed. What else was she going to do? Sit around and mope, and analyse her night with Luke and fume? 'OK, sure. Where and when?'

'Thank you, sweetie, you're a star. It's a fund manager in the West End. Be at 86 St James's Street at nine. You're to report to a Mr Luke Harrison.'

Emily's heart lurched. Her blood went cold and her palms were damp. 'No—wait, Sarah. You know something? I was really looking forward to this week off. Lots of drawers to tidy, windows to clean, that kind of thing…'

'He specifically requested you.'

'Did he just?' said Emily tersely.

'Is there a problem?' asked Sarah.

She closed her eyes briefly and took a deep breath. She was professional. She was an adult. She could handle this. 'Not in the slightest. I'll be there.'

'I knew I could count on you. Bye.'

Emily closed her phone and tapped it against her mouth, a frown creasing her brow.

Anna stared at her in concern. 'You've gone very pale. What is it?'

Emily picked up her glass and took a sip. 'What's with this man?' she said. 'He won me, seduced me, abandoned me—'

'He seduced you?' Anna's voice cut her off like whiplash.

Emily waved a distracted arm. 'Well, not really. Technically,

I suppose I might have seduced him. But that's irrelevant. I don't know what's he's playing at, but it seems I'm to spend the rest of the week temping at Luke's company.'

When Anna recovered from her surprise she shot Emily a conspiratorial smile. 'Interesting… Whatever he's playing at, we'd better draw up a battle plan.'

Professional, polite, detached. Professional, polite, detached.

The words reverberated around Emily's head as the lift zoomed her up to the top floor. But how on earth was she going to be able to do professional, polite and detached when her stomach was churning and her hands were shaking? Any minute now she'd see him again. That thrill currently rippling through her could stop right now. She needed to focus and get a grip. Cool and dignified. That was what she was aiming for. She'd done nothing wrong. He was the rotten coward. She straightened her spine and smoothed her chignon. The lift pinged and Emily fixed a pleasantly neutral expression to her face that she hoped disguised the turmoil that was whooshing around inside her.

Her heels sank into thick cream carpet as she walked to the reception desk. 'Emily Marchmont to see Luke Harrison.'

'I'll tell him you're here,' said the receptionist.

Emily wandered over to the window and stared down at London sprawled out below. Grey streets, teeming with tiny people and mini cars. The hairs on the back of her neck told her he was behind her even before he said her name. Her heart crashed against her ribs.

'Emily.'

She steeled herself and turned slowly round. 'Luke. A delight to see you again.' Thank God her voice sounded steady. He was wearing a beautifully cut navy suit and a pale blue shirt open at the neck, and he was just as gorgeous as she remembered. And, pleasingly, he looked even more tired than she did.

He wasn't smiling. In fact he was looking positively stony. There was a tension in him that made her think of an animal about to pounce. All lean hard muscle beneath that fine wool suit. An image of the two of them entwined on the bed flew unwittingly into her head and for a second she went dizzy.

'Are you all right?' he said coolly.

'Of course,' she replied pleasantly. 'I'm just not too good with heights.'

'You'd better keep away from the windows, then.'

'Ah, yes. Good idea.'

'Thank you for coming at such short notice.' He took her elbow and it was all she could do not to snatch it back. His hand burned through the thin material of her jacket.

'Not a problem. Especially when you're paying so handsomely for my services. Again.'

Luke's eyes narrowed at her saccharine tone. 'How are you?'

'Never felt better. You?'

'The same.' He nodded curtly and led her down the corridor and past a trading room, where a dozen men and women stared at computer screens and talked quietly into phones at each ear. Not for the first time Emily congratulated herself on her chosen career path. Imagine having to work permanently with someone as distracting as Luke.

He opened the door of his office and she went in, taking care not to touch him. Emily looked around the large room, taking in the mahogany table, the ultra-modern cream leather sofa that looked as uncomfortable as it did elegant, and the glass and chrome desk upon which sat a bank of computer screens.

'Nice place. So. Where shall I set up and what would you like me to do?'

Luke walked over and leaned against the edge of the desk while his eyes followed her every movement. 'You can leave your bag there,' he said indicating the sofa. 'There's a pile of filing, and when you've finished that there's some photocopying.'

Emily's spirits sank. If it was any other job she'd be out the door and straight on the phone to Sarah. But if she was honest with herself she didn't want to leave. Despite Luke's filthy mood, it was too good to see him. And it was proving hard to be cool, professional and detached when all she really wanted to do was race over to him and—

Emily swallowed. The bet. Remember the bet, she told herself, fixing a haughty smile to her face. 'I'll get right to it.'

He folded his arms over his chest. 'Aren't you forgetting something?'

Emily raised a quizzical eyebrow.

'My coffee?'

Emily swelled with indignation. How dared he? Of all the outrageous, and probably discriminatory demands… 'Of course,' she purred. 'How do you take it?'

'Black, no sugar. And do have one yourself. The kitchen's down the corridor on the left.'

Emily gave him another hollow smile. 'I'll be right back.'

She turned on her heel and stalked to the door. She could feel Luke's eyes burning into her back as she marched out. She'd give him coffee, she decided, striding down the corridor and swinging into the kitchen. Filing! she thought, as she thrust the kettle under the tap and then switched it on. She hadn't done filing for years. Most of her employers had her putting together presentations, co-ordinating marketing campaigns and managing clients. If he'd bothered to read her CV he'd have known that. By the time she'd finished his filing he'd be sorry he ever asked. He'd never be able to locate anything ever again.

Emily poured boiling water into a cafetière and plucked two cups from the cupboard. And as for photocopying—well, she'd make sure that he'd be recycling paper for years. She pushed the plunger down hard. How was it he wanted his coffee? Black, no sugar? She filled the cups and liberally added milk and sugar to both.

Moving to the other side of his desk to check on his screens, Luke heard the sound of crockery crashing and doors slamming coming from the kitchen. He couldn't prevent a smile spreading over his face. He could almost see the steam coming from her ears. Her expression when he'd mentioned coffee and filing had been priceless.

God, it was good to see her again. Her severe suit, rigid hairstyle and bolshy attitude only strengthened his memory of the softness of her body, the tickle of her hair brushing against his skin, and the incredible way she'd responded to him. Images flooded into his head and he felt himself stiffening.

He frowned and switched his focus to the screens. She looked as though she hadn't been sleeping well, which gave him a sort of grim satisfaction. The need to know why she'd left smouldered in him like an ember. By the end of the day he'd have his answers, and she'd be curling up around him, all sweetness and purring for real, begging for his forgiveness.

Emily carried the two cups of steaming coffee back to the office, where Luke was sitting behind the desk, twirling a pen between his fingers as he watched her. She nearly stumbled under the force of his scowl. What did he have to scowl about? *He* was the one who'd casually seduced her and abandoned her in that hotel in France, and all because of some pathetic macho bet.

She handed him a cup and threw him a challenging glare. 'Your coffee.'

Their fingers brushed and sent sparks of electricity running up her arm. Being in close proximity to this man was dangerous. Especially since the last time she'd seen him he'd been sprawled next to her, naked and all warm hard muscle. Emily swallowed and gave herself a mental kick.

Luke stared down at the cup. 'Thank you,' he muttered with a frown.

'Right. I'd better get on with your filing.'

'Sit down and have your coffee first.'

Emily shrugged and sat on the sofa, which was as unforgiving as she'd thought. If he wanted to pay her for drinking coffee that was his business. She'd drink it extremely slowly, she decided, wrapping her hands round her cup and blowing on the steaming liquid.

Luke's phone rang and he twisted round to answer it. As he rattled off a string of orders to buy and sell various products at various prices at various times, Emily took the opportunity to study him. From the top of his gorgeous head to the soles of those very expensive-looking shoes just visible beneath the desk he was every inch the financial hotshot. Actually, he was just hot, full-stop. He'd look good in anything. Even better in nothing... Emily felt desire start to wind its way through her and bit on her tongue.

Luke put the receiver down and she managed to avert her eyes before he caught her staring at him. *Focus, you fool. Focus.* She blinked and took a gulp of coffee. 'How much money did you just make?'

'About a hundred thousand pounds.'

Emily nodded. The sum was so mind-boggling that she couldn't even begin to get her head round it. 'In around one minute? That's six million pounds an hour. I should raise my rates.' The ghost of a smile played at his lips and then vanished. 'Talking of which, why me?' she said.

'Why you, what?'

'The sudden urgent need for a temp. Me, in particular.'

Luke's expression was unreadable. 'Why do you think?'

Because you wanted to see me again? Emily felt her cheeks flush and cursed the fact that she blushed so easily. 'I have no idea. How did you know where to find me?'

Giving her a searing glance, Luke got up and moved to the window. He thrust his hands in his pockets and stared down at whatever was below the expanse of plate glass. 'Word of mouth. You're very good at what you do. I heard you were the best.'

Emily rose to put her cup on the table. 'I believe that about as much as I believe the reasons you gave for bidding for me in that auction. Remind me again. What were they?'

'Curiosity and the appeal of gallantry.'

'And nothing whatsoever to do with a bet?'

Emily saw him tense. 'Ah,' he said, after a long silence.

She bristled. Was that all he had to say? No apology? No hint of shame? 'Gossip travels fast in the City.'

'And tends to get distorted along the way.'

He could at least look at her. 'So it wasn't a bet?'

Luke turned round slowly. His eyes locked with hers and Emily had to lean against the table to steady herself. It would have been better if he'd stayed staring out of the window.

'You've already discounted the reasons I gave you, and I'm not the type to lust over a photo, so what other reason would I have had?'

Emily went red again. 'I can't imagine.'

Luke flashed her a quick grin that lit up his features and flipped her stomach. 'Did you know that your face is extremely expressive?'

'So I've been told,' she said grumpily.

'I think you're piqued because I didn't bid for you out of some overwhelming desire for your body.'

'Of course I'm not piqued,' she said, injecting as much withering scorn into her voice as she could. 'I'd be utterly horrified if you had.'

'Admit it—your vanity's stung.'

'I'll have you know my vanity is very much unstung. I just don't appreciate being batted back and forward like a commodity between two bored bankers.'

'We're not bankers.'

She arched an eyebrow. 'Rhyming slang.'

Luke registered her jibe with the flicker of a smile. 'It may have escaped your notice,' he said smoothly, 'but that's how an auction works.'

There wasn't much she could say to that. He was right. Her outrage drained away, try as she might to cling on to it. 'You haven't drunk your coffee.'

He walked over to the desk, picked up the cup, took a sip and grimaced.

'How is it?'

'Milky and sweet—just as you intended.'

'Can you blame me?'

Luke continued moving, closing the distance between them, and put the cup down on the table next to hers. He was so close that Emily could smell the soap he used.

'Don't you think you're slightly overreacting?' he said, drawing back a little but still far too close for her comfort.

Probably. 'No.'

'There wasn't a bet.'

'Right.'

'It was more of a competition.'

'That makes me feel so much better.'

'Jack and I have always been competitive, and I like to win. He sent me the link and needled me until I opened it.'

'Poor you.'

For a few seconds they simply stared at each other. The air thickened, crackled, and every inch of Emily's body became aware of his. Luke's eyes bored right through her. 'Actually,' he murmured, 'when I said that your picture had nothing to do with it, I was lying.'

Emily's heart lurched at the look in his eye. 'Oh?' she breathed.

'I'll admit part of it was competitive drive, but the greater part of it was you. I wanted to meet you. I didn't want Jack to have you. And just for once I felt like doing something completely irrational.'

'Why?'

'Too long playing safe,' he murmured.

She wanted to ask him what he meant, but the blaze in his eyes was scrambling her mind. By the time she'd retrieved it he was staring at her mouth and all she could think of was having his mouth on hers. 'Was it part of the competition to sleep with me too?'

There was a long pause, and then Luke sighed. 'Of course not. I slept with you, and you slept with me back, because of this.' He reached out and ran his thumb over her lower lip. Tingles flickered through her.

'You left without even saying goodbye.'

'You hung up on me. I would have said goodbye if you'd bothered to hang around.'

'How was the "emergency" in Dubai?' she said.

Luke raised an eyebrow at her tone and dropped his hand. 'Bad. A new development partially collapsed.'

Emily frowned. 'Was anyone hurt?'

'Only the investors. It wasn't finished. The construction company's share price plummeted. We lost a lot of money.'

'Oh... How did you find out about it?'

'The office called.'

Emily looked at him sceptically. 'I didn't hear your mobile ring.'

'It didn't. It was on vibrate.'

'And that woke you up?'

'I was already awake. I don't sleep much.'

'You obviously have more stamina than I do,' said Emily, thinking how thoroughly he'd worn her out.

'I went back to the hotel as soon as I'd sorted the mess out, but you'd already gone.'

Emily went hot all over. Heart thudding, she stared at him. He sounded genuinely annoyed. Had she got it all wrong? Had she been guilty of assuming that Luke had behaved like a stereotypical male when everything she'd seen of him pretty much indicated the opposite?

Emily suddenly felt rather small. 'Well, of course I'd gone,' she said, folding her arms over her chest. 'I thought it was an excuse. You know—so you wouldn't have to face me in the morning.'

'Why wouldn't I want to face you? I was rather looking forward to a repeat performance.'

'Really?' Emily's eyes widened and her pulse jumped.

'Really,' he said. And then his expression changed, turned harder. 'But you couldn't wait to leave, could you?' His eyes narrowed. 'Why did you leave so hastily? What was it? Did the night we spent together remind you of what you'd lost with Tom?'

'What?' She gaped at him. 'How can you even think that?'

'You were on a plane pretty much the moment you put the phone down.'

'Believe me, Tom was the last thing on my mind.'

'So why did you leave?'

Emily chewed on her lip. 'I told you. I thought it was an excuse. I was having an irrational moment brought on by lack of experience. I've never slept with someone I've only just met. I thought it was a one-night stand and I didn't feel all that great about it.'

Luke's gaze pierced through her. 'I don't do one-night stands.'

'Neither do I.'

He stared at her, and time seemed to shudder to a halt.

'You know what stops it being a one-night stand?'

All she could hear was the sound of her heart thudding in her ears. 'A time-travelling machine?'

Luke shook his head. 'A second night.'

At those words, fire spread through her. 'That would solve it.'

'It would.'

'When?'

'Soon. Very soon.'

She had to bite on her lip to stop herself from trying to persuade him to bring the night forward to right now. 'I'm sorry about the coffee,' she said instead.

Luke tilted his head. 'What other plans did you have for me?'

'Put it this way: you're lucky I didn't get my hands on your diary or your client contact details.'

'You'd better go home before you wreck my business. You'll be paid until the end of the week anyway.'

Emily shook her head. 'I can't let you do that.'

'Yes, you can.'

'Surely there's something I could do to be useful?'

'Actually, there is something…' He took a step towards her. His eyes took on a predatory gleam.

Emily's pulse began to thud. 'Um, no. I don't really think that's such a good idea. We're in your office, for goodness' sake, and I'd never do something like that in return for *payment*.'

'What?' Luke looked bemused, and then grinned. 'What I was actually thinking of was you coming with me to something tomorrow night. But now you mention it…' He stroked his hands up her arms. 'Your idea is much better.' He backed her up against the mahogany table. His hard thighs pressed against hers. His arms slid round her back and moulded her against him.

'You see,' he murmured. 'Incomprehensible though this might be, ignoring it is pointless. And why would we want to deny ourselves the pleasure?'

'Luke…' she breathed, staring at his mouth.

'But you're quite right. We are in my office. My secretary is just the other side of the door. Anyone could come in at any minute.'

Emily gave a little gasp.

'Does that turn you on?' he said softly.

More than he could possibly imagine. But all she could do was give her head a quick shake.

He bent his head and her heart rate tripled. He brushed her mouth with his and then kissed his way to her ear. 'Liar,' he whispered.

Emily was beyond the point of caring.

'I like you all buttoned up like this. Hair tied back, tight little suit. It makes me want to undo you.'

'Undo away,' she breathed, her hands creeping up his chest. The table looked solid enough…

'Unfortunately I have a meeting in ten minutes.'

'So? Plenty of time.'

Luke chuckled and pulled back. 'Not nearly enough. We'll just have to wait. Think of the anticipation.'

'Highly overrated,' Emily grumbled.

'Then think of the rewards.'

'I am. That's the problem.' She picked up her handbag.

Luke laughed. 'I'll pick you up tomorrow at six.'

'Where are we going?'

'It's a charity gala. Black tie.' He paused. 'And afterwards we'll see about eradicating that one-night stand.'

'Is that a promise?' she said coyly.

'I'd say it's non-negotiable in any way.'

She looked up at him from beneath her eyelashes, well aware that her eyes reflected what was going through her mind. Luke wrenched the door open with an obvious effort of will. 'You'd better go, before you make me miss my meeting.'

'You don't know where I live.'

'Yes, I do. Your address is on your CV.'

'So you did read it?'

'Every word.'

'Then the coffee and the filing…?'

His eyes glittered down at her. 'I don't like people walking out on me.'

Emily stared at his mouth and resisted the urge to reach up and kiss him. 'Are you sure there isn't anything I can do now that I'm here? Buy some gold? Exercise an option? Bring down the stockmarket?'

'You're not authorised, and you're too distracting. Besides, you make terrible coffee.'

She sighed and turned to leave. 'Don't tell anyone, but I'm fairly terrible at filing too.'

'I wouldn't worry,' he said, his eyes raking over her so thoroughly she thought she'd go up in flames. 'There are plenty of other things you're good at.'

CHAPTER SIX

EMILY lifted her face to the breeze and the feeling that the evening was going to be magical washed over her. Everything was perfect. She'd found a stunning dress and matching shoes in the first shop she'd gone into and she'd had her hair professionally dried so that it fell in sculpted waves over her shoulders. She'd been transformed into a nineteen-forties siren, and the look in Luke's eyes when she'd opened her door to him had made her feel amazing. Her whole body was buzzing with anticipation and desire.

They were standing with other elegantly dressed guests on the rear deck of a boat that was gliding along the Thames. The buildings on either bank of the river were bathed in warm sunlight and the water sparkled. At least if she did spontaneously combust with desire they could hurl her overboard.

Luke was staring into the distance, his arms resting on the guardrail and his face inscrutable. Emily glanced at him. The wind was ruffling his dark hair. His profile stole her breath for a second. She wished she could read his mind. There were moments like now, when he was deep in thought and his face took on such a bleakness, that her heart clenched. The need to wipe it away pounded through her.

'What's this gala in aid of?'

He twisted round and leaned against the rail. 'Children,' he replied, regarding her blankly.

'What? All of them?'

He gave her a brief smile. 'A number of different charities. It happens once a year.'

'Do you come to things like this often?'

'Often enough.'

The sun lit up his face and Emily shivered with longing.

'Cold?' he asked, shrugging off his jacket and draping it over her shoulders.

The jacket was warm from him, and it was all she could do not to pull it tightly around her and bury her nose in it. 'No, I—' She stopped as she wobbled on her heel. Luke's hands reached out to steady her.

'I would lend you my shoes too, but they might be a bit big.'

'Thank you, but I should be able to manage. I was momentarily blinded by all these jewels on board. I don't suppose they're paste.'

'I'd be surprised if they were.' His eyes roamed over her and she began to burn. 'By the way, did I mention how spectacular you look in that dress?'

'You did.' Emily's inner siren sprang to life. She shot him a smouldering glance. 'Did I mention how easy it is to take off?'

Luke's jaw clenched and his pupils began to dilate. 'Funnily enough, no,' he said.

She moved closer to him. Luke didn't move a muscle. 'I was getting dressed earlier, sliding little lacy knickers up my legs and then slipping my dress over my head and feeling it slithering over me, and do you know what was going through my mind?'

'Advanced calculus?' His voice was taut.

'How you would soon be taking it all off.' Her voice dropped. 'Sliding down the zip, peeling it off me, your hands on my skin.' Luke was staring at her as if he was about to ravish her. No hint of desolation now. 'You know what I really want?'

He gave his head a quick shake.

'I want you to be thinking about undressing me every time you look at me.'

'Shouldn't be a problem,' said Luke, looking as if someone had hit him across the back of the knees with a lead pipe.

'Fair's fair, after all,' she said, running her gaze over him slowly and deliberately, as if she was imagining what lay beneath his dinner suit.

Luke stared at her, his eyes glittering with desire. 'You are pure evil,' he said softly.

'I know,' she said with a smug grin. 'It's great, isn't it?'

'Are you two getting off?'

At the voice of the boat driver they both jumped. Emily swivelled round, and to her embarrassment saw that she and Luke were the only people left on the boat.

The sounds of music and chatter drifted towards them. Emily reluctantly gave Luke back his jacket, and he went ahead of her along the gangplank. When he was on dry land, he held out his hand to help her off. His fingers tightened around hers as they walked up the path towards the huge cream Georgian building spreading out before them. Acrobats leapt and tumbled on the grass to their left. On the right jugglers tossed flaming torches high into the air. A string quartet was playing at the bottom of the marble steps that led up to the building.

'Luke!'

He jerked to a stop. Emily nearly went crashing into him. A man was bearing down on them, smiling widely, and Luke wasn't looking too happy about it.

'I thought it was you. What the hell are you doing here? You haven't been to this for years.'

'Jack,' said Luke coolly. He shook his hand. 'I didn't think this was your sort of thing.'

'I'm broadening my horizons. What's your excuse?' Jack's gaze swivelled to Emily. 'Ah, I see.'

As he looked her up and down in a blatantly appreciative way, Emily decided she really ought to muster up a degree of outrage. But the wicked glint in his eye made it impossible. A slow smile spread across his face.

'Well, well, well—Miss Green Bikini.'

Emily's first instinct was to turn on her heel and take herself and her mortification somewhere they could hide until the boat came to take them back. But she shot a quick glance at Luke, whose jaw had tightened and who very definitely wasn't smiling, and suddenly the whole scenario was intriguing. Undercurrents swirling. Tension crackling. No way was she going to miss any of it.

'I assume you're *greatsexguaranteed*?' She raised a querying eyebrow.

'Who else?'

She tilted her head to one side. 'Modest.'

Jack grinned. 'Talented.'

Emily laughed. 'Outrageous.'

'Thank you.' He gave a little bow. 'Are you going to introduce us?' said Jack, turning to Luke.

'No,' replied Luke.

'Didn't think so,' he said easily. 'Jack Taylor.' He held out his hand and Emily took it.

'Emily Marchmont.'

'You have no idea how delighted I am to meet you.' He gave a theatrical sigh. 'I wish I'd been more persistent.'

'Jack Taylor? As in JT Investments?'

Jack nodded.

'I once worked at your company.'

Jack frowned, as if he was riffling through the bank of women in his head to recall her and failing. 'Really?'

'A year or so ago. I did some temping. You were away on business.'

'You temp?'

Emily nodded. 'I do.'

Jack's gaze flickered to Luke. 'Interesting.'

'Is it?'

'More than you could possibly know.'

He was still holding her hand, and Luke was watching them with narrowed eyes. Smoothly she extracted it and flashed

Jack a wide smile. Even if he was just being polite, he was irresistible.

'Tell me, is there a special place where only beautiful, charming people come from?'

Jack let out a laugh, and Luke's face turned even harder. 'Don't worry about her,' he said curtly. 'She's delusional. Probably dehydrated,' he added pointedly, looking at Jack.

'In that case why don't I look after the very lovely Emily while you go and find some champagne?' said Jack, his eyes gleaming.

The sound of Luke's teeth grinding could probably be heard the other side of the river. 'You're more likely to know where to find it, given the frequency with which you drink it.'

Jack didn't even flinch, just grinned even more widely. 'When I last passed the drinks table,' he said, 'I overheard a couple of people discussing the disappointing performance of their funds and wondering if they shouldn't switch. On your way, Luke, perhaps you could see if you could persuade them to transfer their assets to you.'

'I was under the impression that this was a social event.' The words were spoken smoothly enough, but Emily could hear the trace of steel in his voice.

'When has that ever stopped you? Don't worry. Emily will be in good hands.'

She'd been watching this mini drama unfold with secret delight, but the way Luke was clenching his fists was slightly worrying and the situation needed defusing. She flashed Jack her best smile. 'Would you mind?' she said, batting her eyelids at him winsomely. 'Luke and I were just in the middle of going over our arrangements for after the gala and there are a couple of details we need to clarify.'

Luke went still, and his gaze snapped round to tangle with hers. For a second everything faded, and all she was aware of was the two of them trapped in a bubble of heat, connected by a thread of passion, tightening, drawing them together.

'Isn't that right?' she said softly.

'Absolutely,' he murmured. Tension eased from his shoulders as his eyes darkened.

Jack looked from one to the other and nodded slowly. 'Of course,' he said smoothly. 'In fact, why don't I leave you to discuss your…er…arrangements, and see you at dinner. I'll get someone to revise the seating plan.'

'That would be lovely,' purred Emily.

'See you later.'

Wow, she thought, watching Jack lope off.

'You enjoyed that, didn't you?' said Luke.

Emily nodded. 'Very much. I could get used to being fought over. Especially if the combatants look as good as you two do. Who is he? Besides your partner in internet auction crime.'

'One of my oldest friends.'

Obviously. 'It was quite some display. A bit like stags locking antlers.'

'I'm glad you found it entertaining,' he said dryly.

'I'll probably send thousands of feminists spinning in their graves, but I must admit the whole "woman is mine" thing is very attractive.'

Luke tensed. 'You're not mine.'

Ouch. Emily sensed him withdraw and kicked herself. 'Oh, no—sorry, I forgot,' she said brightly. 'In that case you won't mind if I practise my flirting skills on Jack. He looks like he might appreciate them. He might even be able to give me some tips.'

He shot her a searing glance. 'OK, you're mine for tonight.'

Luke took her arm and they continued up the path. He knew his expression gave nothing away. It was an expression he'd perfected over the last few years. Blank, neutral, shuttered, inviting neither comment nor conversation. And not showing any hint of the storm raging inside him. A myriad of emotions churning around, all so tangled up that he couldn't have identified any one of them even if he'd wanted to.

Going from feeling nothing to this was like leaping from a freezer into a fire. In fact, years of clamping down on his emotions was probably what was making them attack him so strongly now. He felt like a pressure cooker that had been simmering for too long; the lid had sprung open in that damn church and it was going to be hard to push it back down.

He breathed deeply and was struck by a wave of coconut scent from Emily's hair, mingling with her perfume. Bringing her here had not been one of his better ideas. He hadn't thought it through properly. It had been a stupidly rash mistake. The sort of impulsive decision he'd have made five years ago but would never normally make now. He should have taken her out to dinner and sent the organisers of the gala a cheque. Somewhere loud and bright. Somewhere which wouldn't have required her to wear a midnight-blue dress that gave her an hourglass figure and a dangerous attitude.

That would have been the safe thing to do. Emily in that incredible dress and her current frame of mind was not safe at all. On the boat he'd been remembering the last time he'd attended this gala, with Grace, and then Emily had decided to unleash her inner fox and his mind had gone blank.

Then, just when he was dragging his sanity back, Jack—damn him—had shown up, flirting outrageously and no doubt jumping to all sorts of incorrect conclusions. Luke's jaw tightened. It didn't matter what Jack thought. All that mattered was that he kept a clear head and remained in control.

By reminding Emily what tonight was all about, he knew exactly what he was doing, and he was definitely in control.

As they entered the building, Emily could feel Luke trying to steer her straight on, but the women were flowing to a room on the right, whose door was flanked by two burly security guards, and the pressure of his hand on her elbow was no match for her curiosity.

'My goodness,' she breathed, once they'd gone through the doorway. The room had been set up like the jewellery section of a department store. Beneath ancient tapestries stood randomly placed glass cabinets. Each held necklaces, earrings, bracelets, in diamonds, sapphires, emeralds and rubies. Barely aware of Luke, who'd had little option but to follow her, she moved from cabinet to cabinet, peering over shoulders and around bodies in an effort to sneak a peek at pieces that were quite simply breathtaking.

'Another impressive display,' she said, her fingers automatically fiddling with a diamond pendant that hung around her neck from a fine white-gold chain. Beautiful and simple and of highly sentimental value though her necklace was, she couldn't help but drool at what she saw.

She glanced up and saw that Luke's eyes were watching her fingers, so she trailed them slowly over her skin and along her collarbone.

Luke dragged his gaze back up to her eyes. 'Do you see anything you like?'

Emily smiled. 'I like all sparkly things. What woman doesn't?'

'What about those?' He pointed to a pair of huge diamond earrings. Three carats each at least.

She wrinkled her nose. 'A bit on the small side, I think.'

One corner of Luke's mouth twitched. 'Then the sapphires,' he said, taking her elbow and bending over a display cabinet which held a beautiful necklace of intricate white-gold and dark stones. 'They match your dress.'

'So they do,' said Emily. 'Why not? They're quite dazzling.'

Luke nodded at the man standing quietly behind the cabinet, who moved forward, unlocked the door and removed the piece. 'Luke,' she said urgently. 'I was joking.'

He laid it out on a rectangle of velvet and Luke ran his fingers gently over the stones. Emily swallowed.

'Don't worry. We're only borrowing it. The idea is that you wear the necklace, and then when some fool with more money than sense sees how amazing the sapphires are he won't be able to resist buying them.'

'But this must be worth a fortune.'

'Approximately two hundred thousand pounds,' said the salesman.

Emily had to bite back a squeal. 'I can't possibly wear it. What if the catch breaks?'

He shot her a withering glance. 'Our catches don't break,' he said.

'What if I forget and take it home?'

'Believe me, madam,' said the salesman, flickering a glance in the direction of the security guards, 'that won't happen.'

She was running out of protests. And not before time, she thought weakly. One last attempt. 'I'm already wearing a necklace.'

'Take it off.' Luke's voice was low in her ear.

'Undressing me already?' she murmured.

'Yes. I'll look after it.'

Emily reached up to undo the necklace. It was probably safer with him than in the tiny handbag that she was clutching. As she dropped it into Luke's palm, she lifted serious eyes to his.

'Don't lose it,' she said quietly. 'It belonged to my mother. It's very precious.'

'I won't,' replied Luke, slipping it into the inside pocket of his jacket.

'I'm still not sure that this is a good idea.'

'Shut up,' said Luke gently, picking up the necklace and draping it around her neck.

His fingers brushing against her skin as he did it up were warm in contrast to the cold piece of jewellery.

'I feel like a fraud.' His fingers rested on the pulse in her neck and she was sure he must be able to feel it hammering.

'You look like a goddess.'

'More like Cinderella.'

'You'll be leaving before midnight.'

'With Prince Charming?'

'I'm afraid you'll have to make do with me.'

Emily sighed dramatically. 'I suppose I might just manage.'

And then she frowned. 'How will people know it's for sale and not my own?'

'The show starts in fifteen minutes. There are eight other ladies before you, so if I may take your name…?'

Emily's jaw dropped. 'Show?'

'You'll be modelling the necklace on our behalf.'

'In front of all these people? Please tell me you're joking.'

The salesman's expression told her exactly what he thought of that suggestion. 'If madam isn't happy to model the necklace, I'm afraid she'll have to return it.'

Emily ran her fingers over the necklace. To have to give it back now would be unbearable. She nibbled on her lower lip. All she'd have to do, surely, was parade and pose for a couple of minutes. How hard could it be?

'Madam could probably manage a bit of modelling,' she said. 'After all, it *is* for charity.'

'It is indeed.'

She gave her name to the salesman and then threaded her hand through Luke's arm.

'You're dazzling,' he murmured into her ear, with a low voice that turned her knees to water.

Emily shivered. If she wasn't careful all this would start going to her head, and she might start thinking it was for real—the sapphires, the occasion, Luke. And that would never do. This was one night. Maybe a string of one nights. But definitely only a fling. This wasn't real.

As they moved across the marble floor, Luke introduced her to people he knew and brushed off comments about how good it was to see him there. Despite Emily's best efforts, Luke didn't stop to engage in anything other than the barest minimum of small talk. She didn't often find herself surrounded by rich, beautiful people, and she wanted to absorb as much as possible. All the chatter, the exotic scents, the glamour. Even the disdain of a regal silver-haired lady by the pillar, who she could see watching them intently over the rim of her glass.

Emily continued chatting brightly, but could feel the lady's gaze—hostile, frigid, disapproving—and wondered what she'd done to cause it. Could she tell that Emily's dress wasn't designer? Did she know that Emily's bank balance was several zeroes short of a million?

She was just about to ask Luke whether he knew her when he put his hand on the bare skin at the small of her back. She inhaled sharply and all thoughts of the lady by the pillar were wiped from her mind. All she could focus on were the sparks dashing over her skin.

'How long do you think we'll have to wait before we can get round to the non-negotiable part of the evening?' she said, her voice low and husky.

Luke's gaze trapped hers, and she saw her own longing reflected briefly in his.

'Patience,' he replied softly.

'Unfortunately that's never been one of my virtues. Along with abstinence, permanence and prudence.'

'What about endurance?'

'That's something I have in abundance.'

'I think you're going to need it. Off you go.'

She pouted. 'Fed up with me already?'

Luke's gaze dropped to her mouth, just as she'd intended. 'You're being beckoned. Time to strut your stuff.'

Emily was assailed by a sudden attack of nerves. 'Oh, God, I hope I don't do something awful like trip and land in the trifle.'

Luke backed her into a shadowy corner, away from the main group of people heading into the dining hall.

'What are you doing?' she asked, her heart leaping into her throat when she saw the intent in his eyes.

'You've gone a little pale. Not a good look for sapphires.' He slid his hand round her neck and lowered his mouth to hers. Heat poured through her as she melted against him, winding one arm around his waist to keep her upright. His tongue explored her mouth, languidly at first, and then became more and more demanding as the heat built between them. Emily pressed herself closer, greedily taking everything he was offering until he reluctantly broke off the kiss.

'I've been wanting to do that all evening,' he said, drawing in a ragged breath.

'What kept you?'

'Exhibitionism has never been my thing.' He drew back, checked her face and straightened the necklace. 'That's better.'

Emily knew her eyes were sparkling and her cheeks were rosy. But she felt sluggish. Drugged with desire. How in heaven's name was she going to be able to work her legs?

Luke ran a thumb over her lower lip and her breath hitched. He swallowed hard and pulled back.

'Go. Now. I'll see you at the table. Make sure you don't talk to any strange men.'

Emily blinked rapidly to calm her thudding heart and caught the flapping of an arm from a woman with a clipboard and earpiece. 'I promise I'll only talk to normal ones,' she said gravely, flashing him a sexy little smile before heading off to join the group of women decked out in jewellery for sale.

CHAPTER SEVEN

IT WAS all about control, thought Luke, congratulating himself as he twisted away and strode into the dining hall. When he'd drawn back from that sizzling kiss he could have dragged her off outside and bundled her into the nearest taxi, as his body had urged him to. Alternatively he could have ripped her clothes off right then and there and probably got them both arrested. Or he could have watched her cross the floor and allowed himself to be hypnotised by the sight of her smooth brown back.

But, no, he thought, catching Jack's eye on the other side of the room and making his way to their table. He'd resisted. Fought his instincts. Summoned his strength. Demonstrated to himself that he still had the iron-hard discipline he'd developed.

He was in control. No doubt about it.

'Where's Emily?'

Luke's hackles didn't even quiver at the undisguised interest in Jack's voice. 'Part of the jewellery display.'

'I see you took my advice after all,' said Jack conversationally.

'What advice would that be?' Luke nodded and smiled briefly at the other people at the table.

'To have some fun. You've slept with her.'

Luke frowned and his gut clenched. 'Nobody's business but ours,' he said evenly.

'Aha! I knew it,' Jack said, grinning and clapping him on the shoulder. 'And about time too. Welcome back.'

'I'm not back,' said Luke, his face darkening.

'Of course you aren't,' said Jack soberly. 'But it's good to see you with a smile on your face again. Some of the time at least.'

He turned to head round to the other side of the table, a knowing grin twitching at his lips, but stopped suddenly. 'By the way,' he said, tapping the corner of his mouth. 'Lipstick. Not really your colour.'

Luke scowled, picked up his napkin and rubbed. Dropping the napkin back on the table, he pulled out a chair for the lady on his right—the wife of a client—and then sat down as the lights dimmed and music flooded through the room.

As further proof of just how in control he was, he wasn't even going to watch the jewellery parade. No. Instead he was going to focus on the flower arrangement in the centre of the table and mentally go through the list of companies which were due to report their profits over the next couple of days. Then he'd work out how the results would affect the holdings his funds had.

By the time he'd worked out a variety of permutations for his positions the following day, seven women had sauntered past him. Not that he'd been counting.

'Miss Emily Marchmont,' boomed the voice from the speakers, 'is wearing a sapphire and diamond necklace from Cartier. This exquisite piece features thirty sapphires from Sri Lanka, totalling two hundred carats. Their deep blue colour contrasts brilliantly with a sparkling sea of four hundred and thirty diamonds, weighing eighty-four carats.'

Luke took a gulp of wine, sat back, and focused on the flowers. Right. How would his funds perform the day after? His heart slowed and his vision blurred. He rubbed his face and shook his head. And out of the corner of his eye saw her weaving between the tables, shoulders loose, hands on hips as she struck a pose. The spotlight illuminated her skin and the sapphires sparkled against the creaminess. He couldn't drag his eyes away.

His gaze followed her as she came to a stop in front of him and flashed him a haughty, sultry smile that sent a kick of pure lust shooting through him. Her eyes held a challenge, as if she knew exactly how much he'd been trying not to look at her, and then with a toss of her head she continued to the next table.

By the time the lights came up the only positions on Luke's mind were the ones that had featured in that hotel room in France. A light ripple of applause around the table alerted him to the fact that Emily was standing behind him. That and the way the back of his neck prickled.

'How did I do?' she asked.

'Great.' Luke could barely speak, and certainly couldn't stand.

'You were magnificent,' said Jack smoothly, whipping round from his side of the table. 'Let me introduce you to everyone.'

Emily nodded politely and murmured greetings, but inside she was bewildered. She thought she'd done pretty well, all things considered. She'd coped with having all eyes on her when generally she hated being the centre of attention. Even when she'd encountered the silver-haired lady's icy gaze she'd managed not to stumble. So what was Luke glaring about? And why hadn't he got up, the rude man?

'At least I didn't land in the trifle,' she said.

Luke gave her a terse smile, and then turned to respond to something the lady on his other side had said.

His rejection was like a slap in the face, and hurt spiked through her. 'What have I done wrong?' murmured Emily to Jack.

'Nothing at all. In fact you're doing something incredibly right.' Which only added to her bewilderment. 'I've known Luke a long time, and I'd say he's struggling with some serious personal issues.'

Emily frowned. 'He's certainly struggling with manners. What sort of personal issues?'

'Control, among other things.'

'Control over what?'

'You'd have to ask him.'

She glanced down at Luke, who was continuing to ignore her, and allowed pique to swallow up the hurt. 'It doesn't look like he particularly wants to talk to me right now.' Which was fine—because she wasn't at all sure she wanted to speak to him either. She might not be able to stop herself from telling him exactly what she thought of his behaviour.

'No. But that's because I rather think talking is the last thing he wants to do to you right now.'

Luke's shoulders tensed, and then he shot her a quick look so full of desire and promise that it nearly melted her on the spot. Her attention snapped back to Jack and she caught the knowing look in his eyes. 'Right. I see.' And she did. Just as she'd seen the look on his face when she'd posed at the table.

The amused glint vanished from Jack's eyes. 'Make him lose it, Emily. If anyone can, you can.'

She was just about to ask him what he meant when she saw the fierce glare that Luke flashed at Jack. It held a warning that Jack acknowledged with a tiny nod.

'Wine?'

'Yes, please,' she said, resisting the urge to ask him to fill every one of the four beautiful crystal glasses on the table in front of her.

By the time Emily sat down Luke was still so engrossed in conversation that she turned to the man on her left, who was looking at her with admiration. 'You were fantastic,' he said.

'Thank you.'

'I'm Andrew.'

'Emily. Are you in finance too?' she asked.

'I deal in stamps.'

'How fascinating,' she said. 'Do tell me more.'

She'd managed five minutes of conversation on the subject

of philately, which she reckoned was something of a personal best, and had just started on an exquisite plate of tiny squid and truffles when Luke's knee first brushed hers. She nearly jumped out of her seat.

'Are you all right?' said Andrew.

Emily coughed. 'Bit of squid going down the wrong way. Please do go on with what you were saying about the Moroccan Post Office.'

'The Mauritius "Post Office". The world's rarest stamps.'

'Oh, yes—so sorry.'

The continuing pressure of Luke's knee against hers made it almost impossible to concentrate any more. She barely noticed the waiters whipping away the starter and delivering the main course of black cod. Or the champagne ice cream. She couldn't taste a thing.

At one point Luke reached down, ostensibly to pick his napkin up from beneath the table. But his hand landed on her foot and then caressed its way up her calf, creating devastation on her composure. She had to shove a handmade chocolate into her mouth to block the whimper rushing to escape. And then he did it again. He was messing with her equilibrium, her concentration and her mind. Well, two could play at that game.

'Excuse me,' she said to Andrew, waiting until Luke had lifted his wine glass to his lips before putting a hand on his thigh beneath the tablecloth. The hard muscles contracted and Luke nearly choked on the mouthful of wine he'd taken. He swallowed hard and looked at her from beneath hooded lids.

'What?' he said hoarsely.

Emily let her expression collapse into one of irritation. 'Lord, I'm sorry, I can't remember what I was going to say. My mind's gone blank. Don't you hate it when that happens?' she added.

'I think the auction's about to start,' said Tamsin, a beautiful girl who was sitting across the table next to Jack.

'Oh, yes, that was it.' Emily gave her head a quick shake,

as if to say *silly me*, and trailed her fingers higher up Luke's thigh towards his hip and then round. She was itching to see if he was still in the same state that had prevented him from getting to his feet earlier.

His eyes narrowed and his hand tightened around his napkin—beneath which were her fingers.

'Rumour has it you like auctions, Luke,' Tamsin said, shooting him a smouldering glance.

She'd been sending him smouldering glances throughout dinner, thought Emily, as she reclaimed her hand. Pretty much every time they'd exchanged words and even when they hadn't. Totally unnecessary and highly inappropriate, in her opinion.

'Depends on what's up for sale,' he said.

'You can pick up some unexpected bargains,' said Jack with a grin.

'Although I guess you can never be sure that what you end up with will live up to expectations,' said Tamsin.

'I've yet to be disappointed,' Luke said lazily, toying with his coffee spoon.

Emily's heart rocked, and then jumped when the sound of a gavel hitting a table ricocheted around the room. A man was standing at a podium in the centre of the hall and all eyes swivelled in his direction as the lights dimmed.

'Ladies and gentlemen.' His smooth, persuasive tones rang out through the speakers. 'I do hope everyone enjoyed the dinner.' A murmur of agreement rippled through the assembled throng. 'Now we move on to the part of the evening where I encourage you to part with vast sums of money. This evening we have some fantastic lots on offer, which I'm sure will generate huge interest. So, without further ado, let's start with lot number one—a bronze sculpture by one of our leading artists. Who'll start me at a thousand?'

Emily tuned out. The next half an hour or so in semi-darkness would give her much needed time to regroup her thoughts and give her heart a chance to slow to its usual steady self.

What was it about Luke Harrison that reduced her to such a frenzied state? OK, so he was incredibly good-looking and sexy, but so was Jack, and he didn't turn her into a puddle with just a touch. Was it that haunted look in his eyes that she'd caught on a couple of occasions? The hint of mystery? The dry humour? Inner strength?

Who the hell knew? she thought, stifling a sigh. And frankly did it matter? Surely all that was important about this evening was what happened after this interminable gala ended. Emily went warm. Where would they go from here? Her house or his flat? His flat was closer. She closed her eyes. His flat would be modern, she mused. He'd said he had a penthouse, so the views would be spectacular.

She'd kick off her shoes and wander over to take a look. And then maybe he'd walk up behind her and run his hands over her shoulders. He'd slowly slide the zip of her dress down, nudge the straps down her arms and let it slither into a pool of midnight silk around her feet. He'd turn her in his arms and he'd tell her she looked like Botticelli's *Venus*. She'd undo his buttons and push off his shirt and jacket, so that he'd be standing there in just his trousers. She'd run her hands over his chest, maybe grazing his nipple, and then he'd be hauling her against him, kissing her hard and deep, tumbling them to a sheepskin rug, desire taking over, losing control, slick heat, skin, tongues, hands…

Emily's eyes snapped open and she let out a breath. Ohhhh, not good for the heart rate. Not good at all.

She hoped to God no one at the table had noticed she'd drifted off into a fantasy of X-rated proportions. Thank goodness. No sign that anyone noticed anything amiss. She glanced at Tamsin, whose gaze was fixed on Luke. Yet again. She'd better not be having similar thoughts to those that *she'd* just been having, thought Emily. But then Tamsin's eyes flickered to Jack, and Emily's little daydream bubble burst.

She looked at Luke, who was focusing on the man at the podium. He nodded almost imperceptibly. Was he bidding?

Her gaze switched over to Jack. His face was set too. Oh, crikey, she thought, not again. What were they bidding for this time? She craned her neck to see what was on offer, and saw with horror that it was a giant painting of a scorpion.

'What are you doing?' she whispered.

'What does it look like?' Luke murmured, his lips barely moving.

'Sixty thousand. Thank you, sir,' said the auctioneer, pointing his gavel in Jack's direction.

Luke nodded again.

'Are you mad?' she said, trying to keep her voice down.

'I have a lot of white walls that need filling.'

'You can't hang *that* on one. It's awful.'

Luke nodded again.

'You're bidding for it solely to stop Jack getting it, aren't you?'

'Not at all. I wouldn't do anything so childish. It's by a highly sought-after artist and a good investment. Not to mention for a good cause.'

'It's still hideous.'

'I'm feeling reckless.'

'So am I. But, Luke, there's reckless and then there's reckless. If you want something to cover your walls, I'll come and scribble on them. I'd do a damn sight better job than that scorpion.'

'It's not just a scorpion. It's a representation of man's fight against the injustice of capitalism.'

'Hypocrite,' she murmured. 'You're a fund manager. You make your living out of capitalism.'

'I'm a liberal capitalist.'

Emily sniffed. 'Do you like it?'

'It's thought-provoking.'

'It's eye-wateringly ugly. Do you really want it?'

A muscle was ticking in his jaw. She could almost see the battle raging in his head. The auctioneer was looking at Luke expectantly and the room was hushed. After what seemed like hours Luke gave his head a quick shake, and Emily let out the breath that had got caught in her throat.

'Sold,' declared the auctioneer, banging his gavel on the table. 'To the gentleman at table six. Ladies and gentlemen, that wraps up the auction. Many thanks to all of you who bid. Thousands of underprivileged and sick children all over the world will benefit from your generosity.' There was a brief round of clapping and then the auctioneer added, 'The dancing and the casino are now underway.'

Emily was feeling rather stunned. He'd *listened* to her. Luke had listened to her and taken her advice.

'I can't believe you let me have it,' said Jack with a raised eyebrow. You and me both, thought Emily, a bubble of delight fizzing around inside her. 'Too much for you?'

Luke pushed his chair back and languidly got to his feet. 'If you want to hang eye-wateringly ugly art on your walls, Jack, be my guest.'

He put his hand on Emily's arm and bent down. 'Dance with me,' he said softly.

Emily suppressed a tiny shiver. She was a truly terrible dancer, and usually had to be dragged onto a dance floor kicking and screaming, but Luke's voice and his hand had her feeling like Ginger Rogers.

'Excuse me,' she said to Andrew. 'You'd better warn people to steer clear.'

Luke took her elbow and led her off in the direction of the music. Luckily the dance floor was filling up, so there was little room to do anything other than shuffle. Even she should be able to manage that, she thought—until Luke drew her into his arms and her heart began to thunder. The brief respite that the auction had provided was over. He put one hand on her back, the other on her shoulderblade, and need poured through her. Her own hands itched to re-enact her daydream and rip his buttons off, so she planted them safely on his shoulders, well out of reach of buttons.

His eyes raked her face, and then fixed on her mouth in such 'a disconcerting way that she thought she might have a bit of rocket in her teeth.

'What?' she said.

'Nothing.'

'Ah, no,' she said, wagging a finger gently at him. 'You don't get away with that. Only women can get away with the "nothing" card.'

'You saved me eighty thousand pounds.'

'I saved you from having to look at that awful daub every day and from a lifetime of regret at buying it. But that wasn't what you were going to say.'

A smile curved his lips and Emily was transfixed. His arm tightened around her waist even though his tone was mild. 'You seem to be very taken with Jack and Andrew.'

'They're handsome and charming. Who wouldn't be?' The expression on his face darkened. 'Tamsin's a lovely girl, isn't she?' she mused. 'Know her well?'

Luke laughed. Just for a second. But he laughed so rarely, and the sound of it seemed to surprise him as much as her. 'She's a friend of Jack's.'

'She may indeed be a friend of Jack's, but it doesn't answer my question.'

'We went out for dinner once.'

'Just dinner?'

'Just dinner. I may have kissed her goodnight.'

Emily nodded thoughtfully, unable to stop her arms creeping over his shoulders until her fingers slid through his hair and linked together at the back of his neck. 'That would have been the gentlemanly thing to do.'

'I thought so at the time.'

'Just the one kiss?'

'I don't sleep with women on the first date.'

Emily nibbled on her lip. 'So you don't sleep with women on the first date, and you don't do one-night stands. It seems you broke a few rules with me.'

'One, technically the wedding wasn't a date, and two, we've

already established that there is to be a second night. No rules broken at all.'

'Any other rules I should know about?' She arched an eyebrow.

The expression on Luke's face turned serious. 'Only that whatever happens between us can only be short-term. If you remember, I can't offer commitment.'

'Why not?'

'Too messy.'

'You've tried it before?'

'Once.'

'What happened?'

'Not here.'

That wasn't really fair. He'd asked her about her relationship with Tom and she'd told him. Most of it. But the look in his eye prevented her from asking further questions. Emily nodded. 'Well, if you remember, I don't do commitment either.' The last thing she wanted was to go through all the hassle of a relationship again. 'Don't worry, Luke, you've made it perfectly clear on numerous occasions, and I get the picture—really, I do.'

Their discussion was turning so businesslike, and so at odds with the dim lighting and throbbing music, Emily would have stuck her hand out to seal the deal had her hands not been otherwise occupied.

'That's settled, then,' she said, mesmerised by the way his eyes were roaming over her face. 'It's just sex. Pure and simple.'

'There's nothing pure and simple about what happens when we have sex.'

'It's been so long,' she said with a little pout, 'I can barely remember.' She tightened her arms and pulled herself closer, loving the feel of his hardness against her softness.

'You do realise that only one more night isn't going to be enough, don't you?'

Emily nodded. 'How many nights do we have before things become long-term and therefore unacceptable?'

'I've no idea. We'll just have to play it by ear.'

That sounded like a recipe for disaster, thought Emily. How could she stick to the rules if the rules were arbitrary? But it was so lovely moving against him and having his arms around her that she didn't want to break the spell.

'You know what people say about dancing, don't you?' she murmured.

'What do people say?'

'That it's a metaphor for sex. All this closeness. Moving. Touching.'

His hand moved over her back, sliding over naked skin and leaving scorching trails in its wake. 'Is that right?'

Emily bit her lip and nodded. His hand moved lower, his fingers spreading over the top of her bottom, and he pulled her hips to his. 'Like this?'

Emily moaned softly. 'Do you have a sheepskin rug in your flat?'

Luke looked at her in surprise. 'How did you know?'

'This gets better and better,' she said.

The music segued into something more upbeat. 'Now it's getting dangerous,' he said, ducking out of the way of an energetic elbow. He wound an arm around her shoulders and pulled her into his side as they made their way off the dance floor. She could feel the need in her echoing in him and she trembled.

'I'll be back in a second,' she said, extracting herself. 'I think I need to calm down.'

'Then we'll go.'

'So early?' she said, with mock despondency.

The look he fired at her nearly winded her with its intensity. 'It's nearly midnight, Cinders. You and I have a long-awaited appointment with a bed, and I want to get you into it before you turn into a pumpkin.'

Emily felt a beat start up deep within her, obliterating everything except this insane desperate ache. 'Well, in that case I'll be as quick as I can.'

CHAPTER EIGHT

EMILY stared at her reflection. Was that woman with flushed cheeks and eyes that were sparkling as much as the sapphires around her neck really *her*? Her entire body was almost shuddering in longing, and she had to bite down hard on her lip to stop herself moaning out loud at the thought of what she and Luke would soon be up to. She didn't think she'd ever been so turned on in her life. The intensity of what she was feeling, the desire that he whipped up inside her, was slightly scary. She barely recognised herself. Was sex with Luke really such a good idea? She dismissed the rogue thought the moment it entered her head. It was the best idea in the world.

With trembling fingers she unclipped her handbag and extracted her lipstick.

'Excuse me?'

Emily's attention swivelled to the woman who'd appeared in the mirror, standing behind her, and she went still. It was the lady who'd been staring at her earlier. A pearl choker at her throat and heavy diamond studs in her ears, she looked regal and aloof.

'Yes?' said Emily, suppressing an odd flicker of fear and turning round.

'I couldn't help noticing…are you with Luke Harrison?'

Now, there was a million-dollar question. 'I am here with him, yes. Why?' Perhaps this lady was a friend of his mother's. Perhaps this lady *was* his mother.

'Are you stepping out with him?'

'Oh, no, we're just—' Emily broke off and felt her cheeks redden. What could she say? She could hardly tell this *grande dame* that they were planning a long night of hot sex.

'I understand perfectly.'

I really, *really* hope you don't, thought Emily.

'How long have you known him?'

Emily lifted a shoulder. 'Around a couple of weeks.'

'Is it serious?'

Emily resisted the urge to snap that it was none of her business. Anna had spent years instilling in her manners that prevented her from being rude to a woman who was twice her age. 'I don't know. I'm not sure. It's too early to say,' she hedged. The idea of denying it outright was oddly unpleasant.

'He's quite a catch.'

'Er…yes, I guess he is. Do you know him well?'

'Very well.'

The lady didn't say anything further, just carried on staring at Emily with a look that she couldn't make out but that skewered her against the marble.

'Can I help you in some way? Pass on a message? He's out there somewhere if you'd like to say hello.'

The lady shook her head briskly. 'It was you I wanted to talk to.'

Emily frowned. This was becoming perturbing. She glanced round. The ladies' room was now deserted. 'Well, it's been delightful to meet you, Mrs…?'

'Pearson.'

Phew, not his mother. 'Mrs Pearson. But I should probably get back to him. He must be wondering where I am.'

She'd released her grip on the vanity unit and moved to pass when a hand clasped her elbow with surprising strength. 'You know he'll never fall in love with you.'

Emily froze as she felt a shiver trickle down her spine. She wasn't hoping or expecting Luke to fall in love with her, but there was something steely in this woman's eyes that was making her uneasy. 'Why not?' she said carefully.

'Because he'll always love my daughter.'

Emily went cold, and stared down at the huge diamond solitaire on one of the fingers that dug into her arm. Luke was in love with this woman's daughter? So what was he doing flirting and sleeping with *her*? Her brain struggled to make sense of it. He didn't seem the type. From what little time she'd spent with him, she imagined that once in love he'd give everything he had to that one woman. He wouldn't play around with someone else. So that must mean that Mrs Pearson was either mistaken or psychotic and deluded. But psychotic and deluded people didn't usually dress up in pink silk and drip with pearls, did they?

The look in Mrs Pearson's eyes had changed, softened, saddened, and Emily was now filled with foreboding and trepidation. 'Who is your daughter and who are you?' she said quietly.

'My daughter is Luke's wife, and I'm his mother-in-law.'

Emily felt the blood drain from her face. Luke was *married*? Nausea reared up in her stomach. No, that was impossible. He'd said he was single. Had he lied? Emily's brain went into overdrive. No, that didn't make sense either.

'Luke's told me he's single and I believe him,' she said.

'Technically that's true. But he's still married to my daughter. In here,' Mrs Pearson said, patting her chest where her heart was.

Emily frowned. 'I'm sorry, I really don't understand.'

'My daughter died three years ago.'

Emily's legs nearly gave way. Luke was a widower?

'He was devastated. We all were.' For a moment Mrs Pearson crumpled, the fight draining out of her. The lines on her face seemed to deepen, shadows of sadness rushed through her eyes and she looked twenty years older.

'I'm sorry.'

Mrs Pearson pulled her shoulders back. 'I don't need your

sympathy. I just wanted to find out if you knew. Grace was heavily involved in this charity. She was a paediatrician. They used to come to this event together. He hasn't been since she died. I come instead.' She gave Emily a piercing look. 'You can see why I was curious.'

'Yes.'

'Has he mentioned her?'

'No.'

'Well, it's probably a good thing that you know.'

Mrs Pearson left the room and Emily felt as if her world had tilted on its axis. Her heart was pounding and she was trembling. She could forgive the older woman's rudeness. Of course she'd want to know who had taken her daughter's place. Except she wasn't taking anyone's place. Part of Emily wanted to race after her and reassure her that she was no threat. The other part of her was still reeling from shock and she couldn't get her legs to work.

How was she going to be able to go out and face Luke now? How was she going to go up to him and flirt and sizzle and leap into bed with him as he'd be expecting? She just couldn't do it. Her insides twisted. All desire had vanished. What remained was a seething morass of doubt and confusion, tinged with an inexplicable sense of hurt.

Luke broke off his conversation with an acquaintance, glanced at his watch and frowned. Where the hell was she? She'd been in the bathroom for twenty minutes and it was way past midnight. Surely the queue couldn't be that long.

He spied Jack emerging from the casino and excused himself. 'Have you seen Emily?'

Jack raised his eyebrows in surprise. 'Yes, a couple of minutes ago. She was heading over there.' He waved an arm in the direction of the huge doors that led to the hall.

'Thanks,' muttered Luke, shoving a hand through his hair and striding towards the exit. He scanned the hall but there was no sign of her.

'How many times do I have to tell you? I wasn't trying to steal it. I simply forgot I had it on.'

Her voice came from his left, and he strode into the room where the jewellery had been displayed.

Emily was standing in the middle of the room, flanked by security guards—one of whom was gripping her arm. The salesman was punching numbers into a mobile phone.

'What's going on?' Luke's voice was amazingly calm, given the urge he had to yank that security guard off her.

He saw her tense and he frowned. Her face was white, but he couldn't see what was going on in her eyes as she didn't look at him.

'I'm calling my manager,' said the salesman curtly. 'The young lady tried to leave with the necklace.'

'By accident,' she protested. 'It was a simple mistake.'

'We treat all thieves the same. Prosecution is something we vigorously pursue.'

Emily gasped. 'I'm not a thief. If I was I would hardly be trying to make my getaway in a tight dress and three-inch heels.'

'Is there any real harm done?' enquired Luke.

'I suppose not,' replied the salesman grudgingly.

'So she could take it off and give it back to you and you could forget all about it.'

'I have to follow procedure…'

'Will your manager appreciate being woken up at midnight when nothing has really happened?' Luke fixed him with a steely look.

The salesman's face twisted briefly as he assessed the tall, very determined man in front of him. 'I suppose we could make an exception in this case…?'

Luke nodded. 'That would be appreciated.'

The salesman nodded and the security guard released Emily. Her hands shot up to the clasp of the necklace, but she was shaking and her fingers couldn't undo it. Luke stepped forward.

'Let me help you with that,' he said, his fingers brushing

over her skin. She went still, and then flinched at his touch. Luke's jaw clenched as he undid the clasp and handed the necklace back to the salesman.

Then he drew her out of the room. His concern at how much she was shaking mounted.

'You look very pale. What's the matter?'

'I don't feel that great. I might head off. But you stay.'

He frowned. 'If you were so desperate to leave, why didn't you tell me? We were going to go anyway.'

'I'm tired, I have a headache, and I didn't want to interrupt your conversation.'

Luke couldn't fathom what on earth was going on. Why was she avoiding his eyes? And why had she been so desperate to leave that she'd forgotten to give the necklace back? What the hell had happened in the twenty minutes she'd been gone? One minute she'd been shooting him sexy smiles full of promise that had had him wondering whether the venue had bedrooms, and now here she was icy cold. 'I'll take you home.'

'No,' said Emily sharply. 'I just need some air. I'll be fine.'

Luke flinched at the faint note of desperation in her voice. He didn't like it. His expression turned grim and he gripped her arm and pulled her outside. Torches flared down the steps. 'Then we'll talk here.'

'We have nothing to talk about.'

'Non-negotiable, remember?' he said coolly.

'I'm not in the mood.'

'I can see that. But I'm not letting you out of my sight until you tell me what this is all about.'

'I'm tired and I have a headache.'

'I don't believe you.' He noticed the moment the fight drained out of her, and that concerned him more than her coolness did.

'Fine.' She whirled round. 'I've just met your mother-in-law.'

Luke went very still and his face tightened. 'Elizabeth? Where?'

'She cornered me in the Ladies'.'

The pieces of the puzzle slammed into place. 'I didn't know she was here.' How had he not spotted her? He'd always been on good terms with Grace's mother, and still saw her occasionally, so why hadn't she come over and said hello?

'She knew we were. She's been giving me odd looks all evening. Now I know why.'

'What did she say to you?'

'That you were married to her daughter. And that she died.'

'That's right.' Luke raked a hand through his hair and braced himself against the wrecking ball of pain that was about to crash through him.

'What happened?'

'Grace was killed three years ago in car accident. She was driving too fast. It was wet. She skidded and went into a tree.' He switched his attention to one of the torches so that he wouldn't have to see the pity and sympathy in her eyes. He'd had enough of both long ago.

There was a tiny pause, and then her voice came, softer than before. 'I'm so sorry.'

'Yeah, well, it was a while ago now,' he muttered distractedly. Where was the pain? The deluge of memories? The burning anger at the injustice of it all?

'Is that why you were so strange in the church?'

'Strange?' He was feeling rather strange now.

'White-faced, tense, shaking.'

He shoved his hands through his hair. 'I hadn't been inside a church since Grace's funeral. I was expecting it to be grim.'

'And was it?'

'Yes.' But not in the way she probably thought. What had really been grim was the overwhelming guilt that his awareness of Emily had been far stronger than his memories of Grace.

'Why didn't you tell me?'

'I hardly knew you. It wasn't relevant to us.' His gaze swivelled back to hers and he moved towards her. 'It still isn't.'

Emily took a step back and it was like a slap in his face. 'It changes things.'

'Why?' He jammed his hands into his pockets.

'I don't know. It just does.'

'I see.' Luke nodded and felt the shutters slam down over his features. This was precisely what he'd wanted to avoid. Personal stuff getting in the way. *His* personal stuff. 'I'm not surprised you decided to disappear.'

'I wasn't going to disappear.'

'That's what it looked like to me.' His jaw clenched.

'I'm sorry for not coming and finding you. I just wanted some time to process it all. It's quite a lot to take in.'

'You know how I feel about people running out on me.'

'This time you can't give me filing.'

Luke sighed and pushed a hand though his hair. 'No, but I can give you time to think it over.'

Emily nodded. 'I'd appreciate that.'

'Let me know when you've decided what you want,' he said, cursing himself and Elizabeth and coincidence under his breath. 'I'll find you a taxi.'

CHAPTER NINE

EMILY staggered out of bed the next day as dawn was breaking. If things had gone according to plan she and Luke would now be winding themselves around each other and waking up in the slowest, steamiest, most heavenly way possible. Instead she was alone. Her eyes were gritty through lack of sleep, her nerves were jumpy, and she was all tangled up inside.

As she stumbled downstairs she ran through the end of the night before. At last she knew the reason for the haunted look in Luke's eyes, the desolation in his expression, the moments where he seemed to be far away. The death of a beloved wife. Something deep inside her clenched and twisted.

She switched on the kettle and leaned back against the counter while the water boiled. Questions streamed into her head. What had she been like? What had *Luke* been like? How long had they been married? And most of all why hadn't he thought that the fact he'd been married was relevant? That hurt. There was no reason why it should, but it did. Was what they had really so inconsequential?

Well, yes, she supposed it was. What did they really have anyway? she wondered, chewing on her lip. They were simply about sex. Hot, steamy sex. For as little or as long as it took for either of them to get bored. His past didn't need to get in the way any more than hers did. There was no need to torture herself over this.

* * *

Emily sat at her kitchen table, staring at her laptop. She moved it an inch to the right. Now it was bang in the centre of the table. Or was it? No, hang on, it was a little bit too close to the far side.

Oh, come on, she castigated herself. Don't be such an idiot. Just send the damn thing. She'd spent the last two days dithering over whether to phone or to e-mail him. And then, after finally deciding that e-mail was less embarrassing, less intrusive and generally the easier way out, she'd spent hours trying to compose one. She was aiming for brief and businesslike and at long last she thought she had it. She reread what she'd written for the thousandth time.

Dear Luke

I hope you are well. As you must be busy, I'll get straight to the point. I've been thinking about recent revelations and after due consideration, given that neither of us is interested in anything long-term, I don't see any reason why we shouldn't continue as planned. We do, after all, still owe each other one night. If you're still interested, please feel free to get in touch any time.

Emily

All those other incoherent steamy messages into which she'd poured her yearning were safely tucked away in the draft folder and would never see the light of day. She hit the 'send' button before she could back out and got up.

Heavens, it was hot, she thought, fanning herself vigorously with a magazine. Her body temperature was sky high. She'd spent the morning on a lounger in the garden, which in hindsight had been a mistake. The warm sun on her skin had made her think of Luke's hands roaming over her and she'd got all flustered. The heat and the hum of desire coupled with severe sexual frustration were making her restless and edgy.

There was only one place to be when she was in this sort of state. Her shed.

Emily was sitting at her bench when the doorbell rang on the extension. She was in the middle of painting a particularly intricate design onto a huge oval plate, which luckily required every ounce of her concentration. The harder the work the better, she thought. One momentary lapse of concentration and she found herself absently grabbing any stray lump of clay and moulding it into a shape that looked suspiciously like Luke's head.

The heat was unbearable. She'd hoped that the dark, cool shed might have a calming effect on the buzzing inside her. But it wasn't. If anything she was feeling even more feverish.

The bell rang again. She wasn't moving. If it was important they'd come back.

Suddenly a shadow passed across the window, momentarily blocking out the sunlight. There was a quick tap on the door and Luke was standing there, looking big and gorgeous.

Emily gave a quick squeal of shock and leapt to her feet, her paintbrush clattering to the floor and her heart thumping wildly. 'How did you get into the garden?'

'It's nice to see you too. You should lock your gate.'

'Anna said she might pop round later. What are you doing here?'

'You didn't really think you could leave me in limbo for two days, e-mail me like that and not expect me to respond?'

'I only sent it about ten minutes ago.'

Luke held up his BlackBerry. 'I was in a taxi on my way to a meeting. Hardly any traffic.'

He was wearing jeans and a white shirt and had a jacket slung over his shoulder. Despite it being the hottest day of the year, he looked cool, if tired and rumpled. His eyes were glittering dangerously.

'You were going to a meeting in jeans?'

'I've instigated a dress-down Friday policy.'

She had to make a conscious effort not to let her mouth drop open in surprise.

'Aren't they waiting for you?'

'I delegated.'

This, from a workaholic? Perhaps she wasn't the only one being affected by the heat.

'I didn't realise that my e-mail would inspire such haste.'

'You sent me two.'

Emily's heart rate picked up. 'Two? No, I definitely sent only one.'

'I definitely received two.'

Emily went cold. Two? Impossible. Wasn't it? Could she really have been so stupid? Oh, God. What with her nervous energy and the heat, she could easily have clicked on the 'send' button instead of the 'save' button. There it would have sat, innocently lined up and waiting, until she hit the button that actually sent all the messages in the queue.

'There's the one about hoping I'm well, due consideration and recent revelations, etcetera, etcetera,' he said, scrolling down his phone. 'All very promising and interesting, of course—and I *am* well, if you ignore the uncomfortable state of unfulfilled desire. But it was the second one that had me calling one of my team and diverting my taxi. Let me read it to you.'

Emily's cheeks went red. It could be any one of about six…

'No, there's really no need.'

'I'd like to.' He scrolled down further and clicked. 'Here we are… I'll add my own punctuation, as you didn't bother with it.'

'I probably wasn't thinking about punctuation,' she muttered.

'I don't imagine you were,' he said, taking a step forward and bending down slightly, so that he filled every corner of her vision. When he spoke his voice was low and husky, and it grated along her nerve endings. "'This heat, this need, this desire is making me demented. I want to feel you. I want your hands on me. Here. Now. I want you inside me. I need you inside me. I want you to—'"

'Yes, that's quite enough,' she said, burning up inside and out. 'Any good pretending it wasn't intended for you?'

'Wasn't it?'

'Of course it wasn't. It wasn't intended for anyone. I was just…extemping.' Wait, that didn't sound right.

'Extemporising?' One corner of his mouth lifted.

Emily nodded. 'Right, that's what I meant.'

'Whatever you were doing, you can't go round sending e-mails like that unless you're prepared to deal with the consequences.'

He leaned a little closer and the shed suddenly felt far too small. Luke's broad frame took up much needed air, and Emily found herself struggling for breath. She was so hot and flustered. So jumpy inside. Her head went fuzzy and her vision went grey, and then, with a tiny groan, she sank into nothingness.

When she came round she was lying on the sun lounger in the garden beneath a tree. Luke was sitting on the edge of the lounger, staring down at her, concern etched on his face.

'What happened?' she said, blinking up at him.

'You fainted.'

'Odd. I never faint.'

'When did you last eat?'

Emily tried to gather her very woolly thoughts. 'A couple of hours ago.'

Luke gave her a wry smile. 'So I can only assume that it was the shock of seeing me.'

'Probably mortification and heatstroke. Too much time in the sun. Getting all hot and bothered and dehydrated.'

'I must admit you had me worried for a moment. The grey look doesn't suit you.'

Luke was worried about her. Emily tried the thought on for

size and decided she rather liked being worried about. Especially by him.

He was leaning over her, his hands planted either side of her on the lounger. The leaves of the tree rustled and the dappled sun had a kaleidoscopic effect on his face. Light and dark. Colour and shade. The shadows racing over him were making her head swim.

'I'd have thought you'd have women falling at your feet on a regular basis.'

'You're delirious.' The smile playing at the corner of his mouth made her pulse leap.

'Deliciously delirious.' Lord, maybe the sun really had gone to her head. 'How did I get out here?'

'I caught you as you collapsed and carried you out.'

'Anything to get me horizontal?'

'I'd prefer you fully functioning when we finally do get horizontal. How are you feeling?'

'Fine.' Actually, she wasn't. She was feeling rather peculiar—as if someone was slowly replacing her insides with cotton wool.

'You know the cure for heatstroke?'

'Staying in the shade?'

'Removal of clothing.' His eyes glinted at her. 'To encourage heat loss.'

A pulse began to beat deep inside her. 'That would make sense.'

'So we really ought to get you out of those clothes.'

Her gaze flickered over his torso, and she noted with horror that he was smeared in clay. Great splatters and swathes of earthy red all across that white shirt. 'How did you get covered in clay?' she murmured in dismay. How had she not noticed it before? Oh, yes—too busy staring at his face and into those mesmerising eyes.

'You fell at an angle. I landed on your wheel.'

'Did you hurt yourself?'

'No.'

'Clay stains.'

'I have other shirts.'

Emily closed her eyes briefly and pictured him shirtless. Then she shot him a smouldering glance and fluttered her eyelashes. 'It's only fair that if I'm to get out of my clothing you do too.'

'I'm not suffering from heatstroke.'

'Yet,' she said, lowering her eyelids and giving him a slow smile. Her hands reached up and began to undo the buttons of his shirt. 'This really should go into the dishwasher right now.'

Luke grabbed them, putting a stop to her movements. The smile on his face faded. 'You really are delirious.'

'No, I'm not. Just a little fuzzy-headed—and so hot.' She writhed for a moment on the lounger to get some air beneath her.

Luke put his hand on her forehead and frowned. Then he scooped her up as if she weighed no more than a feather and strode into the house. Emily hardly had time to register what was happening, but her arms wound themselves around his neck of their own accord and her head dropped against his chest. He carried her up the stairs, backed into her bedroom and deposited her on the bed.

Oh, yes! she thought, feeling the heat rippling through her. This was what she'd been waiting for, yearning for, ever since she'd woken up alone in that hotel room.

'Stay there,' he said.

'Not planning on going anywhere,' she said, and thought it strange how thick and slurred her voice sounded. Through the haze in her head Emily heard the sounds of taps being turned on in the bathroom and footsteps thundering down the stairs.

He returned with a glass of water and thrust it into her hand. 'Drink this.'

Luke in authoritative, demanding mode was irresistible, so she did as he asked, feeling the icy cold water trickle through her and cool her heated body. And then she tasted a nasty mixture of salt and sugar and nearly threw up. She grimaced and her head swam.

'Yuk, what was that?'

'Take your clothes off,' he said tightly.

Ah, thought Emily. At last. At long last. She fluttered her eyelashes at him and lay back against the mountains of pillows. 'Why don't you do it?'

Luke shook his head with what she thought was a rueful smile. He leaned forward, untied her shirt, and unbuttoned her shorts. 'You're going to have to help me. Sit up.'

'No,' she said, stretching her arms over her head and raising her hips.

'Thought you might say that,' he murmured, lifting her into his arms and carrying her through to the bathroom.

When he put her into the bath of cool water Emily let out a shriek. 'What did you do that for?' she squealed, splashing around in an attempt to get out. But once the initial shock had receded, the coolness of the water was heavenly.

'You, my delirious siren, really do seem to be suffering from heatstroke. Ten minutes in here and then you're going to bed.'

'Are you going to join me?'

Luke sighed. 'You have no idea how tempting that is, but no.' He stood up, thrust his hands in his pockets and turned to head for the wicker chair in the corner.

Emily allowed herself to sink into the water. She felt it seeping up her neck, her chin, then over her mouth and nose and eyes until she was completely submerged. How refreshing. How calming.

Then something gripped the back of her neck and hauled her head out of the water. Panic flooded through her and her hands flailed.

'Emily.' Luke's voice lashed her like a whip. 'Open your eyes.'

She wiped the water out of her eyes and blinked rapidly. His face was white.

'Ow,' she spluttered, twisting her head out of his vice-like grip. 'I was enjoying that.'

'Don't do it again,' he grated, his eyes blazing with anger and what she thought looked like fear.

'I won't,' she said, glaring straight back at him. For a few seconds they stared at each other, and then the anger and panic and concern shifted into something altogether more intoxicating. She saw desire seep into his eyes and her body began to respond. Her nipples tightened and pushed against her bikini top and the sodden fabric of her shirt. Luke's eyes flickered down to her breasts and he jerked back.

Emily felt the wet drag of her clothes against her body. The material felt like sandpaper scraping over her sensitive skin, and every tiny move was exquisite agony. 'Would you mind turning around while I get out of my clothes?' she said huskily.

'After that little stunt, not a chance.' Luke backed away his eyes not leaving her for a second.

Emily shrugged. It wasn't as if he hadn't seen it all before anyway. She peeled off her shirt and deposited it in a dripping heap on the floor. She wriggled out of her shorts and did the same. She twisted her wet hair into a thick rope and drew it to one side. Then she lifted her hands to unclip the straps of her bikini top, dropped it over the side of the bath and sighed in relief as the water swirled over her bare breasts. She glanced at Luke and caught the hungry look in his eye before it vanished. Taking care not to splash any more water over the side, she reached down to slide her bikini bottoms off and then she was naked.

She closed her eyes and sighed with pleasure. The fuzziness in her head was clearing. She heard the rustling of movement, the sound of a towel being pulled off the radiator, and clapped a hand to her mouth to disguise a yawn.

'Can you stand up?' said Luke.

Emily opened her eyes to see him staring down at her. He was standing over the bath holding a towel out, determinedly looking at her face, a muscle ticking in his jaw.

'Of course I can,' she said, frowning. 'I'm not some wobbly waif.' She levered herself to her feet, the water sluicing off her, and still Luke was focusing on her face. She swayed and his arms snapped around her, enveloping her in the towel and lifting her out of the bath.

'I have two perfectly functioning legs,' she muttered. 'But they'll seize up if you keep carrying me everywhere. Where do you get the strength?'

'I play a lot of squash.'

His chest rumbled beneath her ear and Emily shivered. 'So you do have a hobby.'

'I suppose I do,' he agreed, setting her down and rubbing her dry before helping her into the bed and drawing the covers over her. 'Now, get some sleep.'

Luke raked a hand through his hair as he stared unseeingly at his computer screen. Since he'd set it up in Emily's kitchen an hour earlier he'd watched the numbers flicker, brooded about not being in the office, and done absolutely nothing. How could he when all he could think about was Emily, lying naked upstairs? He was going out of his mind. Two days of frustrated waiting. Then that e-mail. Having to put her in the bath and then into bed. He wasn't prone to violence, but right now he wanted to hit something very hard. He rested his elbows on the breakfast bar and flexed his fists.

Judging by the results that were coming though, his traders were doing fine without him. And so they should be. But it was still a disconcerting thought. He rubbed his face. Maybe it was time he took his foot off the accelerator every now and then. His business wasn't going to go down the tubes if he wasn't there every second of the day. He had a first-class team and more money than one man could possibly need. And what was the point of all that money if he didn't have time to spend it? Or anyone to spend it on…?

Luke hit a button on his laptop and the screen switched to the New York Stock Exchange. It was going down. Just as he'd predicted. Good. The kick of satisfaction that he'd got it right was enough of a thrill. He'd survived perfectly well for the last three years without anyone to spend his money on. He didn't need anyone now.

'You're still here?'

Luke looked up and took a sharp intake of breath. Emily was standing in the doorway wearing a short red dress, barefoot and brown-legged, her hair a tangle of curls and sleep still in her expression. 'You startled me.'

'Shouldn't you be at work?'

'They're managing without me.'

She smiled and he felt his body tighten. 'That must be disappointing.'

'Very.'

'I'm sure Anna would have come if you'd rung her.'

The thought hadn't even occurred to him. 'How are you feeling?'

'Much better. Thank you for looking after me.'

'No problem.'

'I was an idiot to stay out in the sun so long.'

'Yup.'

She walked over to him, and with every step she took his blood pressure increased a notch. 'The bath and the sugary salty water... How did you know what to do? When you're not storming the financial markets do you moonlight as a doctor?'

'My talents don't extend to nursing victims of heatstroke. I rang the local clinic after you fainted.'

'You certainly have a fabulous bedside manner.'

'I'm now supposed to check your heart rate,' he said hoarsely.

Emily took his hand and put it on her left breast. 'Feel anything?'

Luke frowned and moved his hand up to hold his fingers against the pulse at the base of her throat. He checked it against his watch.

It was racing.

'Normal,' he said curtly.

'I'm sorry for scaring you,' she said softly.

'You didn't scare me.'

'How can I make it up to you?'

'Don't worry about it.'

'I know we're not doing long-term, but would you like to stay for supper?'

'Fine.'

'Why don't I put that shirt in the washing machine?'

'Not necessary.'

Emily smiled that little smile of hers that turned his brain to putty. 'I think it is. I still ache. You read my e-mail. You know what I want. I know you want it too.'

'You're not well,' he said gruffly.

'I'm fine. Honestly. Look—even my legs are working properly.'

She gave a twirl and dropped into a curtsey, to demonstrate just how steady she was on her feet, and then rattled off a couple of tongue-twisters. 'I can even walk in a straight line.'

She walked over to the freezer perfectly balanced. Then she bent down to take what looked like a couple of steaks out. From the lack of lines beneath the flimsy dress it looked as though she wasn't wearing any underwear, and Luke's resistance snapped.

'All right. I'm convinced.'

Emily straightened so slowly that he could see every movement beneath that red silky material. His mouth went dry as she put the steaks on the worktop and turned round. He was so hard he ached. His erection strained against the zip of his jeans and he didn't think he'd ever felt pain like it. The need to feel her body beneath his hands and sink himself inside her nearly floored him.

And then she was walking towards him. No, walking wasn't the right word. Sashaying. That was the only word to describe the way her hips were gently swaying from side to side as she closed the distance between them. Her eyes darkened and her breathing slowed.

'So, we have a couple of hours before the steaks defrost. What are we doing to do with ourselves?'

His jaw clenched. 'I'm sure we can come up with something.'

She stopped just beyond his reach and arched an eyebrow. 'Monopoly? Charades? Read a good book?'

Luke's heart raced. He unfolded his arms and stared at her. 'How about a game for only two? This has been going on long enough. Any longer and I may suffer permanent damage.'

'Well, we can't have that,' she murmured, resuming her sauntering until she was pushing herself between his knees.

'Are you sure about this?' he grated.

'Of course. Everyone has baggage. But ours needn't affect this in any way.'

'I couldn't agree more.'

Then her fingers were fumbling with his shirt buttons and his hands were on her hips, tugging her towards him. His fingers dug into the soft flesh of her buttocks and he pulled her against him to where he ached and throbbed. By the time she got to the last couple of buttons her fingers were shaking so much that she couldn't undo them.

'Oh, sod it,' she muttered. 'It's ruined anyway.' Her hands gripped the thick white cotton at the bottom of his shirt and yanked it open. The buttons spun into the air and bounced off the work surface.

'And I do have plenty of others,' he said, his eyes boring into hers. 'Just not here. You've effectively rendered me captive.'

'So you have to comply with my every whim?'

'It does look that way.'

'Then I demand that you kiss me.'

'I think I might like being held captive by you,' he said. He leaned forward and planted a kiss at the base of her throat, where her pulse was hammering. And then another lighter kiss just above. He carried on until she was whimpering.

'Luke.' It came out as a groan, a plea full of longing. And just when she thought she could bear it no longer his mouth settled on hers. A slow, languid kiss that made Emily's blood start rushing through her veins. Her hands slid over his chest, smoothed over the muscles of his shoulders and then wound around his neck, pulling him closer, deeper, as if yearning to fuse with him.

A pulse began to throb deep in the centre of her, and she moaned beneath the movement of his lips, loving the taste of his mouth and the feel of his tongue lacing with hers. She pushed his shirt off. He deepened the kiss and she shuddered. She couldn't stop her hands running over his back, curling in his hair, gliding over his shoulders, gripping his hips so that she could grind hers against them.

Emily's heart raced. Her body was out of control, and an exquisitely painful pressure was building inside her that only he could assuage. Her fingers fumbled at the button of his trousers. With a groan of frustration she wrenched her mouth from his and looked down to see what she was doing.

As her fingers brushed over his engorged flesh Luke inhaled sharply. He stilled her trembling hands and guided them behind her back. 'No,' she moaned. 'I want you inside me now.'

'Soon.' He stood up and backed her against the breakfast bar. 'We have a lot of making up for lost time to do.'

'No, now,' Emily whimpered, but he took no notice. He lifted her up so she was perched on the edge of the bar, placed her palms on the cool granite behind her and pressed her back. He pushed the straps of her dress down and the bodice slithered to bunch at her waist, exposing her swollen, heavy breasts to his hungry eyes. Luke dropped a trail of kisses along her jaw and down her throat, cupping one breast in his palm and rubbing his thumb over her nipple. Emily went dizzy from the sensation, darts of pleasure shooting through her, and then his mouth continued, caressing down gently over the slope of her breast and closing over her other nipple. Hot and wet, his tongue flicked over the tight bud and she let out a groan of pleasure.

His hand trailed lower, his fingers gliding over the skin of her thigh under the hem of her dress, creeping higher until they found what they were looking for. Emily's hips jerked and she bit on her lip to stop herself crying out when he slipped a finger into her hot wetness and stroked back and forth, finding and rubbing her clitoris. Bursts of pleasure rippled out from her core and she groaned, panting wildly.

She tried to stop the sensations. She wanted to hold on until he was inside her, properly inside her, filling her, swelling, pounding into her. The image was too much. The pressure too great. His fingers too relentless. Demanding too much. Waves of desire rolled through her. She could feel herself tensing. Her breath came quicker, her heart thundered as the coil inside her wound tighter and tighter. And then his lips found hers, his tongue plunging into her mouth, mimicking what she really wanted, and she shuddered, tensed, and splintered into millions of tiny shafts of pleasure.

'So unfair,' muttered Emily when she finally got her breath back. 'Damn you and your control.'

He kissed her hard, setting her on fire all over again, pulling a condom from his back pocket with one hand and drawing her dress up over her head while Emily grappled with his jeans. She was desperate for him to get as naked as she was, so that finally she could feel him, all of him, touching her body from head to toe.

And then he was standing in front of her, all glorious tanned muscle, his erection thick and big. Emily shivered.

'Cold?' Luke murmured, rolling on the condom, his face tightening with the effort of clinging on to his control.

She shook her head quickly. 'Burning up.'

'Me too.'

Locking her ankles around his waist, he slid his hands along her legs, gripped her hips, and entered her with one long smooth thrust. She felt herself stretching to accept him and great bursts of pleasure began to throb deep inside her.

His hands steadied her hips as he set a rhythm that had her pelvis tilting and drawing him in deeper. Emily groaned, slipping one hand behind her to support her and wrapping the other around his neck. He crushed his mouth against hers, their tongues duelling as his pace increased, pushing her closer and closer to the brink.

Emily wrenched her mouth away and drew in great gulps of air. 'Oh, God,' she panted. How was it possible? France had been amazing—unsurpassable, she'd thought. But this—this was something else. She felt she was about to break open. Surely her body couldn't stand so much intense, deliriously mind-blowing pleasure. He withdrew and she moaned with despair. And then he drove into her one last time, hard and up to the hilt, and she came apart, spiralling into blissful oblivion, convulsing around him as waves of delight crashed over her, feeling him climax a second after her, pulsing into her.

Her hand drifted down over his shoulder and she could feel his heart hammering. He ran his hands up her sides, round her back, and cradled her head against his shoulder. They stayed like that, locked together, for a couple of long, hot minutes while their breathing regulated and their heart rates subsided.

Then Luke gently withdrew from her and she missed him immediately. Reality intruded, and the realisation that they were standing in her kitchen naked in the middle of the afternoon made her want to giggle.

Luke picked up her dress and slipped it over her head. She sat there, legs dangling, watching him as he discarded the condom and thrust his feet into his jeans. Was there anything sexier than a man in nothing more than a pair of jeans? She wanted him again. How was it possible? And then he was pulling on his shirt and buttoning up what few buttons there were. Surely he wasn't leaving…

'Where are you going?' Her voice was still husky and unsteady.

He picked up the foil packet and turned it over in his fingers. 'We're going to need more of these. A lot more.'

The relief that flooded through her nearly knocked her off the breakfast bar. 'No need. I have hundreds. Well, maybe not hundreds,' she said, when Luke raised an eyebrow, 'but certainly enough to last until supper—and they should just about be within their use-by date…'

'Good,' said Luke, shooting her a smouldering stare and unbuttoning his shirt. 'Where?'

A broad grin spread across her face. She levered herself off the worktop. 'Come with me,' she said, taking his hand and leading him towards the stairs.

CHAPTER TEN

PULLING a blanket over her shoulders, Emily watched Luke at work at the barbecue. As she regarded him over the rim of her glass of wine she was struck by how very at home he seemed, lighting the coals and blowing on them so that they'd catch. His shirt had long since been abandoned, and she had a glorious view of his back, bending and twisting, the muscles rippling beneath tanned skin. Strong, capable shoulders—the sort of shoulders that could bear a great deal and had no doubt already done so.

She was insanely attracted to him. But there was something else too. Something deeper, entangling her emotions and making her giddy. He flashed her a smile over his shoulder and her heart gave a little lurch, as if to warn her of how much danger it was in.

'While we're waiting for this to get ready will you show me your pottery?'

Emily chuckled. 'Are you asking to see my etchings?'

'I've already seen your etchings quite a few times this afternoon.'

Lord, and didn't she know it? Lethargy had taken hold of her, and she wasn't sure if she could summon the strength to get up and cover the short distance to her shed.

'Right now I'd like to see what you get up to at the end of the garden.'

'OK.' Emily stretched and got up. 'When I'm not communing with the fairies I make all sorts of things. Jugs, bowls, plates, vases. Big ones. Didn't you see them earlier?'

Luke shook his head. 'Too busy making sure you didn't hit your head.'

Generally she didn't allow anyone in her shed. Not even Anna. But Luke had already been in it once, so what harm would there be if he went in again? This time she'd keep a good few metres between them, she resolved, stepping through the door and switching on the light. He bent his head and followed her.

'This is what I do.' She swept an arm wide to indicate the bench cluttered with an assortment of brightly coloured pieces.

Luke surveyed her bench, and then picked up a bowl and turned it slowly in his hands. Emily's throat tightened as she banked down the urge to snatch it back. He was staring at it assessingly and she felt it personally. She hadn't asked for his opinion, but suddenly she found it mattered. Which was not only annoying but also potentially dangerous. If he was critical in any way, she'd jab him with her paintbrushes.

'These are good—very good.'

Pleasure and relief spun through her. 'Thank you.'

'Have you sold any?'

'No. I give them away. Mainly to Anna and to friends.'

'Have you ever had a show?'

'No. Why?'

'You should.'

She let out a resigned sigh. 'Let me guess. You think I should see if I can make money from it.'

'It's really none of my business, but if you can make money doing something you love it does seem the ideal scenario.'

'Hah! I knew you wouldn't be able to resist.'

'What do you mean?'

'Someone who eats, sleeps and thinks work would never understand doing something just for the sheer pleasure of doing it, with no monetary gain.'

'That's rather harsh,' he said, sending her a slow smile.

'I've just spent the entire afternoon—a weekday afternoon, I might add—doing something just for sheer pleasure with no monetary gain.'

'I'm not talking about sex,' she said, feeling herself grow hot. She took a deep breath and a step back.

'Pity.' Luke turned his attention back to the bowl. 'You could sell these for a fortune. All those people with minimalist flats and acres of white walls.'

'That's true. As someone with lots of white walls, what would *you* choose?'

Luke scanned the room. 'The vase,' he said eventually.

Emily followed the direction of his gaze and had to hide her surprise. It wasn't what she would have expected him to choose. She would have thought he'd go for something solid and dark and useful, but the three-foot-high vase he'd chosen was delicate and curvy, and painted in turquoise and green with splashes of red. It had taken her ages to make and then decorate and was one of her favourite pieces. She'd had to hire a kiln specially to fire it.

'Good choice,' she said, nodding.

'Wouldn't you like to sell your work?'

'Not really.' No one she knew would pay good money for an oversized, garishly painted bowl.

'Or simply exhibit it?'

'That's just vanity. And can you imagine how embarrassing it would be if no one came?'

'They would. How could they not?'

Emily felt something unfurl deep inside her and swallowed hard. 'I should tell you that this is a conversation I've had on a regular basis with my sister for a number of years. Whatever you say won't make the slightest difference.'

'There's no reason why it should, but if you don't take risks, you don't get rewards.'

God, if only he knew, she thought. She was reaping rewards with him—but at what risk? 'Do you take risks?'

'Taking risks is part of my job.'

'And personally?' She stared into his eyes and heard her breathing shallow.

'Are you trying to distract me?' Luke murmured.

'Yes. Is it working?'

'No.'

'Should I faint again?'

Luke glowered. 'Don't you dare.'

'I reckon the barbecue should be ready by now,' she said.

While Emily headed into the house to fetch salad and baked potatoes, Luke tossed the steaks onto the grill and watched them sizzling and spitting. She was wasted as a temp. She ought to be creating great vibrant pieces that would shake people like him up. Not that it mattered to him what she did with her life one little bit.

'Hmm, that smells good,' she said brushing against him. 'And the steaks don't smell too bad either.'

Luke grinned. 'How do you like it?'

'Rare, please.'

'In that case they're done.' He put the steaks on a plate that was obviously one that she'd made, and took it to the table on the patio. A candle flickered between them and light spilled out from the kitchen.

'Did Anna show up while I was asleep?' Emily said, helping herself to salad.

'No.'

She dropped the salad servers into the bowl and went red. The way she blushed so easily was oddly captivating. 'What?' he asked, filling her glass.

'I hope she didn't pop by while we were…you know…'

'Testing the strength of your kitchen units?'

'Precisely,' she mumbled, and took a gulp of wine.

'I hope she didn't either.' Luke had a sudden image of a furious Anna bearing down on him with a meat cleaver. 'She's very protective of you.'

Emily nodded. 'She has a right to be. She brought me up.'

'What happened to your parents?'

'My mother died having me, and my father died when I was fourteen.' Luke saw something flicker in her eyes before she averted her gaze. Only briefly, and a different man might have missed it. But he caught the guilt mainly because he recognised it.

'She brought you up on her own?'

Emily nodded. 'There was no one else to do it. Only one set of grandparents, and they lived in Australia.'

'So Anna was what? Eighteen? Nineteen?'

'Twenty. She was at art college, but she dropped out and did accountancy exams instead.'

'That must have been a hard decision,' he said, slicing through his steak but watching her closely.

Emily shrugged, and once again the guilt was written all over her face. 'She had me to look after. So she passed her exams and took a job with regular hours and a steady income.' Then she smiled. 'Luckily she turned out to be really good at her job and loved it.'

'A bonus.'

'I already feel terrible about what I made her sacrifice. Can you imagine how much worse it would be if she'd hated it?' She shuddered.

Luke sat back. 'It must have been tough on you too.'

'I was a brat.'

'Understandable.'

'Unforgivable,' she corrected. 'I owe her a lot. Now she has my gorgeous brother-in-law and the twins and she's equally good at looking after them.'

'They're very lucky.'

Emily nodded and put her fork down. 'I know I moan about her bossiness and interfering, but really I don't know what I'd do without her.'

The admiration, love and respect that she had for her sister and her family was apparent in her voice. Here was a little group of people having life hurl terrible things at them and they'd weathered it all. By leaning on each other. Whereas he'd weathered his own storms alone. By choice. It had started out as the only way to avoid the sympathy and the pity, and it was now a habit. He felt a pang of something that he suspected might be envy and his chest squeezed. His solitariness had never bothered him before. He considered it to be a strength. So why should he doubt it now?

'What do you fancy for dessert?' said Emily, shooting him a smile that had his body tightening in response.

The need to wrap himself around her gripped him, but this house, so warm and inviting, was suddenly stifling. Luke shoved a hand through his hair and got to his feet. 'I should go.'

Emily's heart practically ground to a halt. He was going? Now? After the afternoon they'd had? It was barely nine o'clock. She'd just fed him and he was leaving? Puff went her dreams of the two of them waking up and making slow, leisurely love before breakfast. She could feel his retreat as strongly as if he'd actually vanished. That blank look on his face and the shuttered expression in his eyes was horrible.

'I need the cover of darkness to hide the fact that my shirt is ripped and covered in clay.'

'Of course. I do apologise.'

Had she gone too far, spilling out her relationship with her sister? Had all that been too personal, given the fact that they weren't having a relationship? God, she was hopeless at this sort of thing. It was precisely why she didn't do casual flings. She tended to forget the rules. Could she persuade him to forget the past half an hour and promise not to mention anything personal ever again?

Emily blew out the candle as Luke headed inside and picked up his shirt. He really was leaving, she thought despondently as she watched him do up what few buttons there were. And by the looks of things he couldn't wait.

But just as she was about to let him know exactly what she thought of his behaviour he swung round and strode towards her. He yanked her up against him and gave her a brief searing kiss that left her reeling.

'Go and get your toothbrush. Underwear is optional.'

Absurd delight bloomed in her chest. 'You want me to come with you?'

'Unless you have plans for the weekend?' he said.

Her heart raced and she grinned. 'No, no plans whatsoever. What about you?'

'My plans have just changed. And I still have your necklace at my flat.'

'Oh, wow,' said Emily, crossing the room to the wall of windows that looked over the rooftops of Mayfair.

'I thought you didn't like heights,' said Luke as he went into the kitchen.

Emily flushed. 'That was before,' she murmured. Heavens, was it really less than a week ago that she'd been storming around his office?

'What would you like? Wine or coffee?'

'Coffee, please. I spy a thoroughly pointless gadget over there in the corner that looks far too clean and complex to have ever been used. I'm intrigued.'

'It's not a thoroughly pointless gadget. It's the Rolls-Royce of espresso makers.'

'Have you ever used it?'

'No. I have a kettle.' Luke started searching through his cupboards. 'Somewhere.'

'Have you ever used *anything* in this kitchen?' she said, noticing how shiny everything was.

'The fridge.'

'How long have you lived here?'

'Three years,' he muttered, finding coffee in one of the cupboards.

Since he'd been alone… That made sense, thought Emily, her gaze sweeping around the apartment. It was as modern and sleek as she'd imagined it would be. Open plan, immaculate

white walls, angular furniture and glossy wooden flooring.
The only hint of Luke's personality were the bookshelves,
which were stacked with an eclectic mix of military histories,
biographies and well-thumbed thrillers. There was no sign of
his wife at all.

'Your coffee's on the table.'

'Thank you,' said Emily, turning around and seeing where
he was staring. 'It looks good, doesn't it?'

The turquoise vase was standing in the corner of the room,
a splash of colour against the otherwise rather clinical deco-
ration. She'd been about to get in the taxi when she'd acted on
an impulse and dashed into the garden to get the vase to give
to Luke.

He frowned. 'It does.'

'Much better than a six-foot by four-foot scorpion.'

'But not nearly so worthy.'

'I'll have you know my vase represents the female struggle
for emancipation.'

'Aren't you a bit late for that?'

'Not at all,' she declared airily. 'It's an ongoing struggle.
And apart from that it was also a very efficient chaperone in
the taxi.' The vase had sat between them like a prim maiden
aunt.

'Too efficient. But before we set about reversing that, I'd
better go and get your necklace.'

Luke disappeared, and Emily caught sight of something
that looked like a photo album. She pulled it off the shelf and
opened it, half wondering whether she wasn't intruding.

Her heart thumped. It was full of photos of Luke and the
woman Emily could only assume had been his wife. She had
brown wavy hair and was lovely.

But what struck Emily most were the pictures of Luke.
Luke laughing and smiling. Looking relaxed and happy and
carefree. The opposite of the cool, controlled man he was now.
Her heart twisted. What would it take for him to be like that
again?

'Here you are.'

She looked up guiltily, expecting him to be angry that she'd been nosing around, but his expression wasn't giving anything away. He merely handed her her necklace, which she slipped into her bag.

'I hope you don't mind me looking.'

He shook his head sharply.

'What was she like?'

'Beautiful.'

Naturally. 'Did you love her very much?'

'Yes.'

Emily's heart squeezed. It was her own fault for asking.

'Does it still hurt?'

'Sometimes,' he said, not looking at her.

'Does it get any easier?'

There was a long silence. A crease furrowed his brow. 'Slightly,' he said at last.

Emily closed the album and replaced it on the shelf. She walked back to the window and stared out. She pitied the woman who fell in love with Luke. He was clearly still haunted by the memory of his wife. A woman he'd loved deeply and no doubt passionately. Who'd died before age and life had left their mark. What living woman could ever compete with a memory like that?

It was just as well that she was only interested in him for incredible sex and nothing more.

Luke didn't want to think about Grace. He didn't want to think about the fact that he'd stopped thinking about her all the time some time ago. He didn't want to think about the absence of the ache and start wondering when exactly it had gone away.

He hadn't brought Emily here to talk about Grace. He'd brought her here for dessert.

He moved so that he was standing behind her. He swept her hair to one side, bent his head and brushed the back of her neck with his mouth.

'You're trembling,' he said softly.

'Probably,' she murmured.

'What from?'

'Anticipation,' she whispered.

'Of what?'

'The fulfilment of a fantasy.'

'Care to elaborate?' he said, pushing his hands under her T-shirt, sliding them up over her skin and drawing it over her head.

'I should be wearing my blue dress.'

His hands closed over her shoulder, and then he moved one down to cup her breast. It moved lower still, to dip below the waistband of her jeans. Emily leaned back against him and let her head fall back. He ran a trail of kisses up the side of her neck and then turned her round.

'I can't imagine a fantasy that involves you wearing any clothes,' he said against her jaw.

'I wasn't wearing it for long.' She ran her hands over his chest and rubbed her thumb over his nipple. His skin contracted at her touch.

'You said something about a sheepskin rug. Does that feature in the fantasy?'

'It has a key role,' she said solemnly.

'How key?'

'Tell me where it is and I'll show you.'

'It happens to be in my bedroom.'

'That's good. What I have in mind for it would be most uncomfortable in the bathroom.'

'Why would I have a sheepskin rug in the bathroom?'

'Kinky?'

'Do I look like the kinky type?'

She smiled slowly. 'You've just been undressing me and touching me in front of a floor-to-ceiling, wall-to-wall window. You have the potential.'

CHAPTER ELEVEN

EMILY woke from the depths of sleep to the sound of her mobile ringing. 'Hello?' she said groggily.

'Hi.' The panic in Anna's voice wiped the sleepiness from her head and she sat bolt-upright.

'Anna, what's wrong?'

'It's Charlie. He's got a temperature. A high one.'

'What's the matter with him?' She rubbed her eyes and got out of Luke's bed.

'I don't know.' Anna sounded on the verge of tears. 'He's pink, and there are spots on his chest. Oh, God. I need to get him to hospital, but David's away again, damn him, and I don't think I can manage with Peter too.'

'Calm down, Anna.' Emily scooped up her clothes and tiptoed into the sitting room. She had never heard her sister so shaken and her blood turned to ice. 'Have you called an ambulance?' She pulled on her jeans and somehow got herself into the rest of her clothes.

'Yes, it's on its way, but it's going to be at least half an hour.'

She glanced at her watch. One a.m. At this time of night there wouldn't be any traffic.

'I'll be with you in a quarter of an hour. I'll stay with Peter while you go with Charlie to hospital. Try to stay calm. I'll be there as quickly as I can.'

She hung up and dropped her mobile into her bag. She jumped as Luke appeared in the doorway, already in his jeans, running his hands through his hair and dragging a jumper over his bare chest.

'I'm sorry for waking you. What are you doing?'

'Taking you to wherever you need to be.'

'Luke, it's one o'clock in the morning. I can get a taxi.'

'Not happening. Don't even bother trying. Let's go.' He picked up his keys and ushered her out.

Emily was too worried and too grateful to argue. Within minutes they were speeding through the dark empty streets of central London. Cocooned by cream leather seats and glossy wood, Emily tried to imagine the terror that must be going through Anna's mind. She'd never heard such panic in her sister's voice. Anna had always been the strong, reliable one. To hear her crack like that tore at her heart. If something was to happen to Charlie…after all they'd suffered… It didn't bear thinking about. She couldn't imagine what Anna was going through. And no mother of her own to fall back on. As the familiar pang of guilt reared up in her, Emily had to unclench her fists and remind herself that it wasn't her fault.

Luke pulled up outside Anna's house and Emily scrambled out of the car. The front door was flung open and Anna was standing there, white-faced and red-eyed.

When she saw Emily she crumpled into her arms. Emily hugged her sister fiercely and stroked her hair.

'Oh, God, Em. What if it's meningitis?'

'Shh. The ambulance will be here soon. They'll do tests. He'll be fine.'

'He's so tiny. And so red and blotchy.'

'Where's your husband?' said Luke, moving them all into the house and closing the door behind him.

'Milan. I wish he was here. Bloody conferences.'

At that, Emily found herself smiling slightly. That flash of normal Anna was reassuring.

'When's he due back?'

'He's on the next plane over, but it doesn't leave for another six hours.'

'I can get him here quicker than that,' said Luke, pulling his mobile out of his jacket. 'Give me his phone number and I'll sort it. Emily, make tea.'

'What's he doing here?' asked Anna, watching Luke twist away and punch numbers into his phone.

Emily followed Anna into the kitchen. 'It's not important. What's important is that we get Charlie to the hospital.'

'A bit of a distraction wouldn't go amiss right now,' said Anna shakily.

She'd do anything she could to take some of Anna's worry away, and if it meant spilling the beans about what she'd been up to, so be it. 'He was with me when you called.'

'Doing what?'

'Helping me put up curtains.'

Anna gave her a watery smile. 'That's what it looked like when I dropped by on Friday.'

'You didn't!'

'I did. Briefly.'

'When?'

'Just in time to see you rip his shirt off.' *Oh, no.* 'Don't worry, I didn't hang around. Have you been with him since then?'

Emily nodded. The day before they'd woken up late and then gone out for breakfast. They'd strolled up to Hyde Park and Luke had taken her out on the Serpentine in a rowing boat. They'd spent the afternoon window shopping before the crowds of Saturday afternoon shoppers had sent them back to Luke's flat and its huge bed. Where they'd stayed until Anna's phone call.

'Are you in love with him?'

Emily hid her face in the cupboard as she searched for the tea. 'Don't be ridiculous. Of course not. You can't fall in love with someone in a matter of days. It's just sex.'

'I fell in love with David within half an hour of meeting him.'

'That was different. David's heart wasn't encased in ice, and he fell for you too.'

'Yes, but—' Anna broke off when Luke walked into the kitchen.

'The ambulance is outside,' he said. 'Your husband will be here in a couple of hours. A car will meet him at the airport to take him to the hospital. Let me know if there's anything else I can do.'

'Thank you, Luke—for everything.' Anna gave him a peck on the cheek, scooped Charlie up and headed outside. 'Look after my little sister.'

Emily stifled a groan. Didn't she have more pressing things on her mind? She ran after Anna and gave her and Charlie a big hug. 'Good luck.'

'Thank you for coming to my rescue.'

'You know I'd do anything for you, but I really, *really* wish you hadn't told Luke to look after me. It's not that sort of thing.'

'Maybe not, but are you sure it's just sex?' murmured Anna, giving her a brief wan smile before climbing into the ambulance.

Emily watched the ambulance whizz down the street, a deep frown etched on her forehead. Sighing deeply and wrapping her arms round her waist, she turned and headed back to the house.

'Luke, I know this isn't the way you planned to spend the weekend, so please don't feel you have to stay.'

'I don't.'

Her heart twisted. 'OK, that's fine,' she said, nodding numbly and thinking it was anything but.

'Emily, I'm not going anywhere. We'll wait until your sister's husband gets here.' He glanced at his watch. 'He shouldn't be too long.'

'He could be hours.'

'Then that's how long we'll wait. Stop being difficult.'

He put his arm round her shoulders and led her back into the house. Emily had a sudden vision that had her heart thundering and her mind swimming. What if this was her house? Their house? And it was their baby upstairs asleep? Oh, God. Where had that image sprung from?

Heading upstairs to check on Peter, she told herself to snap out of it. She was tired, emotional and vulnerable. This wasn't like her. She crept into the twins' room and stared down at the sleeping baby. A wave of something odd swept through her, and she jerked back before she could give in to the urge to bend down and inhale the soft sweet smell of him. What on earth was wrong with her?

She whirled round, and in her haste to grab the baby monitor knocked it to the floor. She froze. There was a heavy silence, and then Peter let out a wail. Emily winced at the sound. If she remained really still and didn't even breathe maybe he'd go back to sleep. Another scream tore through the air. No such luck. The wailing continued. Emily stared down at Peter's red, screwed-up little face, at those little arms and legs kicking, and covered her ears with her hands.

'What's going on?' Luke's voice next to her made her jump.

'Ugh, that noise. It cuts right through you.'

'Standing there with your hands over your ears won't stop it.'

'It hurts. Do something. Make it stop.'

'You're a woman.'

'And?' she said challengingly.

'Don't you have an innate knowledge of what to do?'

Emily raised an eyebrow. 'The maternal instinct bypassed me. And I'd never have pegged *you* as a chauvinist.'

Luke rubbed his eyes. 'I'm not.'

'So you do it. You pick him up. I don't know how to.'

'Have you never picked up your nephews?'

'No.'

Luke bent over the cot and lifted up the screaming child. 'Never babysat?'

'Anna wouldn't trust me to.'

He held the baby awkwardly, but although Peter's legs were still kicking furiously the volume of his cries went down a notch. 'Are you sure? You were the person she rang this evening.'

That was true. But still…

'That's enough,' he said firmly. 'Be quiet.'

The child went still, stopped mid-scream and stared at him. Luke stared back.

'You're a natural,' said Emily, watching him put the baby back down and pull a blanket over his now calm little body.

She stood on one side of the cot and Luke stood on the other, both looking down at Peter. Then Emily's eyes met Luke's, and that image of a happy family attacked her again. Her knees trembled and she twisted away, making a great fuss over searching for and picking up the baby monitor.

'Don't you ever want children?' Luke asked as they headed downstairs.

'Not particularly. Not all women do, you know.'

'Why not?'

Emily shrugged. 'Too much responsibility. Too much pain. Can you imagine the terror that Anna's going through right now?'

'Sort of.'

Emily saw him shudder and kicked herself. 'Do *you* want children?'

His eyes narrowed. 'No.'

'Why not?' If he could ask her, she could ask him.

'I've no intention of marrying again, and I'm neither irresponsible nor careless.'

'There are far too many children in the world as it is.'

'Quite.'

'That's what I tried telling Tom, but he wouldn't listen.'

'Is that the real reason why you split up?'

She nodded. 'He couldn't understand it. Initially he didn't want them either, but then he changed his mind and thought he'd be able to change mine.'

'He clearly didn't know you at all.'

Or perhaps he had. Her resolve seemed to have become

strangely unsteady in the last hour or so. 'I'd better see if there's any news on Charlie,' she said, walking into the kitchen to call her sister.

When she hung up Luke was on the sofa in the sitting room, his legs stretched out and his eyes closed. The deep comfortable sofa with Luke at one end was tempting, but she headed for one of the armchairs by the fireplace. God, he was gorgeous, she thought, and then admonished herself for the rather inappropriate timing of her thought. He'd been amazing tonight. He'd stopped Anna and herself turning hysterical. His strength made her heart wobble.

'Come and sit by me.'

'I thought you were asleep.'

'Nearly. How's your nephew?'

'He's going to be fine.' Relief was still whipping round inside her. 'It's a rash. Some sort of allergy, apparently. Anna did tell me what it was called, but it's late and it was a long, complicated name and I've forgotten.'

'Good.' His eyes flickered open. 'Come here,' he said again.

Emily sank onto the sofa and leaned into him, absorbing his strength and his warmth. She breathed in deeply and felt her tension unravel.

Moonlight was streaming in through the patio doors when she jolted awake. For a moment she was disorientated, and then a number of things filtered into her consciousness. The sound of the front door opening. The steady thud of Luke's heart beneath her ear. Her arm thrown over his chest. The feel of his body entwined with hers as they both sprawled on the sofa.

Emily blinked. Gently she unwound her arm from his chest and her legs from his. Luke jerked awake, and she found herself staring into his eyes. What she read in their unguarded depths she couldn't make out. But it was something that made her heart lurch.

After a couple of heartbeats that seemed to last for hours, Emily pushed herself up and straightened her clothing. Luke rotated his shoulders, flexed his arms, and ran his hands through his hair.

Emily was getting to her feet as her brother-in-law entered the sitting room. He looked haggard. 'How's Charlie?' she said, her voice rough with sleep.

'He's absolutely fine,' he said, his gaze flickering over Luke, 'but they're keeping him in for a while longer just to make sure.'

Emily smiled for the first time in what felt like ages. 'I'm so glad. This is Luke Harrison. Luke—David Palmer.'

'I have a lot to thank you for,' David said gruffly, shaking Luke's hand.

'Don't mention it.'

Emily could see the two men sizing each other up and approving of what they saw. It gave her a warm, fuzzy feeling inside that she wasn't sure she wanted to identify.

'How's Peter?'

'Asleep.'

'Any trouble?'

'None whatsoever. He was as good as gold.'

'It's late. You head off. Thanks Em, Luke.'

They stepped out into the dark night. When they got to the car Luke opened the door for her and she got in. 'Let's go back to your house,' he said. 'It's closer and I'm shattered.'

She gazed up at him. 'Thank you for everything you did tonight.'

Luke shrugged. 'I know what it's like to feel helpless and utterly alone. The least I could do was get David back as quickly as possible.'

'Who was there for you when Grace died?' she asked softly.

'No one.' He shut her door and walked round the bonnet to the driver's side.

Emily went dizzy. She wanted to pull him into her arms. She wanted him never to hurt again. She wanted to protect him, look after him, find out everything there was to know about him. She wanted to go to bed with him every night and wake up with him every morning. She wanted to make love with him for ever. Oh, Lord, she thought, her heart hammering as he got into the car. Once again Anna had hit the nail on the head. She was head over heels in love with him.

CHAPTER TWELVE

'YOU'RE very quiet,' said Luke.

'Just thinking,' Emily murmured, staring out of the passenger window at the dark terraced houses.

'What about?'

'Things.'

'That's almost as bad as "nothing".'

'Mmm.' Things were certainly bad. She was in love with Luke and probably had been from the moment he'd agreed to accompany her to the wedding when he clearly hadn't wanted to. She was in love with a man who'd sworn never to love again. Who was in all likelihood still in love with his dead wife and only saw *her* as an entertaining diversion.

But *was* it just sex? Surely he must feel something else for her, however remote and tentative. Would he have bothered to take her to the gala if it was just about sex? Would he have looked after her when she fainted, and would he have done all he'd just done if it was only about sex? Or was she once again hoping to see something that wasn't there?

Because it was highly unlikely that he'd have changed. If she wasn't going to fall into the futile trap of thinking he would, she should get out now. Thank him for his help, go into her house, lock the door behind her and protect her heart from any further damage. Now was the time to do it. As he was parking the car outside her house. All she had to do was yank the passenger door open, tumble out, race up her path and she'd be safe. The initial agony would be brutal, but brief. She'd get over it. In about a hundred years.

Her heart thudded and her mouth went dry. Her hand reached for the handle. Could she really do it? She glanced over at Luke one last time and her stomach turned itself inside out. He was watching her, his face serious, his eyes gleaming with simmering desire, and Emily realised she had no more chance of resisting him than she had of becoming a world dance champion. She was doomed.

Every step up the path with him was a step towards insanity and probably unimaginable pain, but she couldn't stop. Her body and her heart craved him. It was out of her control. She would take what she could and worry about the consequences later.

'Just how tired are you?' she asked, dropping her keys on the hall table and turning to him.

Luke's eyes darkened. 'Exhausted. You snore.'

'I don't,' she said indignantly. 'Do I?'

'It's more of a snuffle.' He flexed his shoulders and winced.

'A massage might help to ease those muscles.'

'It might.'

'Did I ever tell you I once temped in a massage parlour?'

'That wasn't on your CV.'

'Well, it wouldn't be, would it?' she said softly. 'It might give employers the wrong idea.'

'It's giving *me* wrong ideas,' he said, tugging her into his arms and kissing her deeply.

Somehow they tangoed up the stairs and into her bedroom, still locked in each other's arms. When they parted Emily's breathing was shaky and her whole body was trembling. 'Take off your clothes and lie on the bed face down,' she said.

'All of them?'

'All of them.'

'Be gentle.'

A minute later she'd stripped to her underwear, and Luke was naked and prone, in her hands and at her mercy. God, he was magnificent. Was it because she now realised that she was in love with him that he seemed so much more…*everything*?

She straddled him, put her hands on his shoulders, and felt his muscles clench beneath them.

'Relax,' she whispered, bending down to his ear.

'Impossible,' he muttered.

'You'll see.' She kneaded and pressed her way over his body until she felt the tension ease from him. Then her touch changed, and the kneading and pressing became caressing and stroking.

'How does that feel?'

Luke mumbled something that sounded like 'amazing' into the pillow, but it could well have been 'agonising'.

'Now the front. Turn over.'

'Can't.'

'No need to be embarrassed.'

'I'm not,' he said, lifting his head a fraction. 'You're on top of me.'

So she was. Biting on her lip to stop a giggle escaping, she moved just enough to allow him to turn over, and then she was astride him again. Only now his erection was pressing insistently against her and she nearly lost her mind.

Luke was watching her with a look in his eyes that said *You've got me where you want me, so now what are you going to do with me*? Emily knew exactly what she was going to do with him. He'd said she needed to take risks. Well, she about to take a massive one. She was going to try and make him lose control.

As if he could read her mind, he clenched his jaw and his eyes glittered. She leaned down, laced her fingers with his and kissed him slowly and thoroughly. The low-burning flame inside her burst into life. His fingers tightened around hers and she felt a tremor rush through him. She dragged her mouth from his and trailed a line of hot kisses down his neck and his chest. Her tongue flicked over his nipple and she heard his sharp intake of breath. She disentangled her hands from his as she continued kissing her way down over the muscles of his stomach to where the hard length of him was straining.

'Emily…' he said raggedly.

'Shh.'

Their gazes locked for a second before she lowered her head and took him into the warm wet heat of her mouth.

She heard him groan, and could feel the effort he was making not to thrust upwards. The hand that wasn't tangling in her hair was clutching the sheet. She swirled her tongue around the tip of his erection, licking away the tiny bead that had formed there, and then slowly closed her mouth around the length of him again.

Luke shuddered beneath her as she carried on. His hips were jerking and she sensed he was close. Emily lifted her head and slithered her way back up his body wriggling out of her knickers as she did so. His eyes were almost black, and the eerie silvery light accentuated the strained planes of his face. He dragged her against his chest and kissed her fiercely, igniting the heat deep within her.

'You're very good at that,' he grated.

Emily pushed herself up on her palms and drew her knees up to straddle him. She reached behind her and unclipped her bra. 'I've read a lot of books.'

'I'd love to know the sort of books you read.'

She laughed softly and leaned over to the bedside table. She rolled a condom onto him and lowered herself slowly, until he was entering her inch by incredible inch.

'Oh, God,' he muttered as she began to rock slowly and sensuously, the moonlight outlining her shape as she moved over him. She bent forward to brush her nipple against his lips, and then leaned back before he could take it in his mouth. And all the time she was looking into his eyes. Boring into him, as if trying to get a glimpse of his soul. She was bewitching him. His heart was pounding. His body was getting tight. She was squeezing gently as she moved up and down him and he could feel his control slipping away. He tried to cling on, but his body was clamouring for the ecstasy that only she seemed able to give him.

Emily shook her hair back as she writhed, and it was the most erotic thing he'd ever seen. Barely aware of what he was doing, he moved one hand from her hip to grip her thigh and moved the other to her waist.

In one smooth move he flipped her over, so she was lying on her back and he was rearing over her, still buried deep inside her. Her eyes registered brief shock, and then glazed over with desire. Her lips were swollen and red and wet, and set something off deep within him—something primal. The need to possess was so overwhelming that he felt himself slide under. He felt as though he was drowning. Her eyes held his. He couldn't break away even though he desperately wanted to. He couldn't stop. His arms were shaking with strain as he drove into her over and over again. Her hips came up to meet each thrust. Her breathing was ragged. Her hands roamed over his shoulders, his back, over his buttocks, pulling him deeper into her, driving him closer to an edge that was sharper and higher than anything he'd ever experienced.

What do you want from me?

Let go.

No.

Yes.

She let out a cry and clamped around him. Her back arched off the bed but still her eyes held his. Her abandon, her complete release, wiped out the last vestiges of his control. As she convulsed again and again he thrust harder and faster, his body coiling, tight, the pressure building.

He stared into her eyes.

Yes.

He shattered. His mind went blank as he emptied himself into her.

Luke sat in the armchair in the corner of her room and watched Emily sleeping. He was transfixed by the soft rise and fall of her chest, the occasional twitch of her mouth, that funny little snuffle that she made from time to time. He couldn't fool himself any longer. This game with Emily was becoming more than a game. If he was being honest with himself it had never been a game. He'd just chosen not to acknowledge it.

The feelings twisting around inside him were more than mere lust. He didn't know what they were, but he was very afraid of what they might become. He'd tried to keep it light and casual. But this last time something had changed. Her touch had been different. She'd made him lose control. If she'd asked him to stop he wouldn't have been able to. Her hands, her mouth, her eyes, had been telling him something he really didn't want to know.

His chest squeezed. He suddenly felt as though he couldn't breathe.

He shoved a hand through his hair and his eyebrows snapped together. They'd spent the last two days together, and now he couldn't imagine her not being around. It couldn't be allowed to continue. He wouldn't get himself into the same situation as before, where he'd cared for someone, loved someone, only to have them snatched away. The memories of that time after Grace's death were too hard to bear. The hollow ache inside him. The wretched desolation and loneliness. The guilt that he was still alive. He wouldn't be put through that again, and he wouldn't put himself in a position where it might happen.

Emily was aware she was being watched long before she opened her eyes. She could tell by the way her skin tingled and desire began to awaken inside her. She stretched out an arm and felt the space beside her cold and empty. Her eyes snapped open and she saw Luke sitting in the corner, looking far too big and brooding for the delicate chair. What was he doing over there and not in her bed? And why was he dressed? That was something that needed to be remedied right away.

'Hi,' she said, with a wide sleepy grin.

'Hi.'

His tone had her fully awake. She watched him warily, but he didn't move from the chair and his expression didn't alter. The intensity of his gaze made her uneasy. She didn't know why, but she was suddenly scared.

'Last night, did you ask me to stop?'

What an odd question. 'Of course not,' she said, drawing the duvet up to her chin as if it would provide some sort of defence against whatever was happening. 'Why would I have asked you to stop? I wanted it to go on for ever. Come back to bed.' She tried to send him a smouldering smile, but her heart wasn't in it.

His jaw clenched. 'We need to talk.'

The smile slipped from her face and she felt as though someone had stabbed her with an icicle. 'What about?'

'Us. This.'

His eyes were devoid of emotion. This wasn't the Luke she'd come to know over the past few weeks—the Luke who'd protected her from gossips, given her his coat when she was cold, flirted with her and made such magnificent love to her. This Luke was cold, distant, and she didn't like him one little bit. Her insides felt as though they were being torn in two. The massive risk she'd taken had failed. She made him lose control and now he was punishing her for it.

'Is there any point?' she said, shrinking further beneath the duvet. 'I know what you're going to say, Luke.'

'What am I going to say?'

She closed her eyes for a second. 'You think we should stop seeing each other.'

There was a long pause that told her she was right, damn him. Her heart cracked. A tiny part of her had so hoped that she'd be wrong.

She opened her eyes and forced herself to look at him and continue. 'And I agree.'

'You do?'

Thank God she had a thick duvet. If he could see the way she was shaking he'd never have believed her.

'Absolutely. It was only supposed to be temporary, after all, and it's no longer a one-night stand, so it's probably best if we make a clean break of it. Short and sharp.' Like the knife slicing though her.

'Why?'

Because I'm an idiot for thinking you'd change. Because my heart is breaking. Because I love you too much, and to have to listen to your reasons and your excuses would break what's left of me.

'Because it's what you want, isn't it?'

He sighed and raked a hand through his hair. 'Yes.' He levered himself to his feet. 'I have to go.'

It was only though sheer will-power that she managed to keep her face from collapsing. Inside she was splintering. 'OK.'

Luke walked over to the bed. He placed his hands either side of her head, leaned down and gave her a long, drugging kiss. A goodbye kiss. And then he was gone. The front door slammed and Emily knew beyond all doubt that she'd never see him again.

A wave of nausea hit her and she clapped a hand to her mouth. Flinging back the duvet, she raced to the bathroom and retched and retched. When that was over, she splashed water over her face, threw herself onto the bed and promptly burst into tears.

Over the next few days Emily sank into black despair. She cancelled her work on the grounds of sickness, dimly aware that she was letting Sarah down but unable to summon up the effort to care. She felt wretched, mangled, distraught. Luke didn't want her. She'd offered him everything and he'd rejected it. With an aching heart, she went over and over it in her mind, analysing every conversation they'd had, tormenting herself with wondering whether there was anything she could have done differently. But, whatever she'd done or not done, sooner or later the result would have been the same.

The weather had been largely sympathetic. Great heavy, humid clouds hung over London, suiting and fuelling her misery perfectly. But after a thunderstorm the night before the sun was now out, spilling into her room and demanding that she pull herself together.

Sighing heavily, Emily levered herself and her bruised heart out of bed and went into her bathroom. She flung a cursory look at herself in the mirror, did a double take and then shrank back in horror. Her skin was so pale it was almost grey—except where a rash of spots had broken out—her eyes were red, and her hair was lanky and dull.

Well, that was what a week of no vegetables, fruit or sleep but gallons of misery and chocolate ice cream could do to a girl.

Supposing Luke came back and saw her looking like this? Idiot, she berated herself. There was zero chance of that happening. Still, it wouldn't hurt to get dressed and tidy up a bit, would it? Her bedroom carpet was barely visible beneath the blanket of scrunched-up tissues and her bedside table was piled high with empty ice cream cartons. If she carried on like this for much longer, her bedroom would end up as an exhibit at the Tate Modern.

Emily dragged herself into the shower, threw on some clothes and, feeling marginally better, headed down to her shed. It was time to make some changes. She'd make herself forget about Luke. She'd get over him. She wasn't the first girl in history to have a failed love affair and she wouldn't be the last. She'd just have to find some of that inner strength to support her in the days to come. And she'd find it at her wheel, just as she always did. The feel of the clay squeezing through her fingers and the hypnotic whirl of the wheel would soothe her nerves and wipe her mind.

Mind you, she didn't have much space left. If she didn't do something about her pottery soon she'd run the risk of having the whole lot topple on top of her and ending up fossilised beneath the resulting mountain.

She really should have an exhibition, she thought, eyeing her work critically. Some of it *was* good enough. She could easily make more. As excitement began to creep into her head, her mind swam with possibilities. Images of her lovely creations in a beautiful gallery. All the rich and famous gasping in awe over her talent and the sheer impact of her work.

She'd show Luke. She didn't need him. She'd become an overnight success, receive rave reviews and meet a heavenly man with no issues who would fall madly in love with her.

Hmm. Earth calling Emily. How did one go about sorting out something like an exhibition? Maybe Anna could help, she thought, reaching for her diary. She opened the book and ran her eyes over the pages. How long would it take? She tapped her pencil against her teeth. Did galleries have waiting lists? And how much would it cost? Could she really do it? Of course she could. With a bit of backbone.

She flicked over the pages and her heart skipped a beat. Then it slowed right down and a shiver raced down her spine. As if in slow motion she turned the pages back and went cold. Oh, God. There it was. A week ago. The circle around the date.

All thoughts of an exhibition vanished. Her heart hammering, Emily told herself to calm down. Maybe she'd noted the dates down wrong. With fumbling fingers she turned back through the pages to double-check. The dates were accurate.

No need to panic. There could be a thousand and one reasons why she was seven days late. Even if she was usually as regular as clockwork. Stress. That was a good one. The last week had been stressful, to say the least. And what about the fainting episode? Maybe her blood pressure was still out of balance? Maybe it was all that ice cream?

Just please, please let it be *anything* other than… Bells started clanging in her head. The diary fell from her fingers and thudded onto the floor. Oh, Lord, no. It was unthinkable. Impossible. She and Luke had used condoms every time they'd had sex. Every time. There was no way she could be pregnant. There *had* to be some other reason.

As if on cue, the smell of varnish hit the back of her throat and her stomach revolted. Suddenly drenched in an icy sweat, Emily stumbled out of her shed and threw up into a flowerbed.

Trembling violently, she staggered into the house and gulped down a glass of water, fear gripping her whole body at the mounting evidence. Unable to stand the uncertainty any longer, she grabbed her handbag, flew out of the house and raced to the pharmacy at the end of the road.

Three minutes. That was what the box said. The box was wrong. Thirty seconds was all it took for the second blue line to appear and for her life to come crashing down around her ears. She was pregnant. Her head went fuzzy and she collapsed onto the sofa, curling into a shaky, shivery ball.

Terror wound itself round her insides, creeping through her, twisting, wrenching, until it reached her brain and exploded into sheer white blinding panic. She squeezed her eyes tight shut and started shaking even more.

Then, thankfully, her brain shut down and she spun headlong into denial.

CHAPTER THIRTEEN

'YOU look sickeningly brown,' said Emily, smiling wanly as she bent down to give her sister a hug.

Anna hugged her back. 'You're looking peaky. Are you all right?'

Not really. She felt battered and bruised, like a tiny yacht that had been tossed around on the high seas by a tropical storm. 'Fine. Tired, that's all. How was the holiday?'

'Corfu was heavenly. Just what we needed after the panic with Charlie. But I don't want to talk about my two weeks of glorious sunshine, empty white beaches and delicious food. I want to hear what you've been up to.'

Emily sat down and wondered what Anna would say if she told her the truth. A week of excruciating unhappiness followed by an attack of twenty-eight years' worth of fear and guilt. It was all too raw. 'Potting,' she replied instead, watching the twins crawling on the grass.

Anna raised her eyebrows. 'I wouldn't have thought you'd have time.'

Emily ignored her suggestive tone. 'I'm thinking about having an exhibition. Displaying some of the stuff I've produced.'

'Really? That's amazing.'

'It's no big deal. My shed is getting cluttered, that's all. But I might need your help with sorting a space and things.'

'Whatever you want, darling,' she said, picking up a menu and scanning it. 'What's brought about this change of heart?'

Emily shrugged. 'Nothing important.'

Anna's head snapped up and Emily averted her eyes from her shrewd gaze. 'How is the lovely Luke?'

'I have no idea,' she said, her throat threatening to close up. 'Rotting in hell, with any luck.'

Anna dropped the menu. 'You're not seeing him any more?'

Emily shook her head.

'What happened?'

'I fell in love with him.'

Anna smiled triumphantly. 'I knew it.'

'And so he ended our affair.'

Her smile vanished. 'Why?'

'I don't know. He backed off.'

'Oh, darling, I'm sorry. No wonder you're looking peaky.'

'Today is a good day. I haven't cried for a whole hour.'

Anna squeezed her hand. 'This calls for wine.' She waved at a passing waitress.

'Bit early for me,' said Emily awkwardly. 'I'll have some camomile tea.'

The order given, Anna sat back and fixed her with a penetrating stare.

'What are you looking at me like that for?' said Emily warily.

'You're pregnant.'

Her stomach churned. 'What makes you think that?'

'You have that look about you.'

'The sick-to-the-stomach-and-utterly-shattered look?'

'That's the one.'

'That could be misery.'

Anna shook her head. 'It's not just misery.'

Emily shuddered. 'Is there any point in my denying it?'

'None whatsoever. I'd simply have to try and ply you with alcohol and prawns and brie until you ran out of excuses.'

'In that case, you're right.' She dropped her head into her hands as her chest tightened and a tremor ran though her.

'Oh, my God, this is so exciting! The twins will have a little cousin. How many weeks are you?'

'I'm not sure.'

Anna frowned. 'You have been to see a doctor, haven't you?'

Emily looked up and bit her lip. 'Not yet.'

'But you should be looking after yourself.'

Emily swallowed painfully. 'I only found out a few days ago. Anna, don't judge. Please.' She was on the brink of tears.

'Of course not, darling. How are *you* taking it?'

She was carrying the baby of the man she loved. Her heart skipped. A little girl or boy who'd have dark hair and green eyes. Or maybe blue eyes and fair hair.

A child who might well kill her the same way she'd killed her mother. The spark of delight was swept away by a tidal wave of pure fear. 'Badly. I will go and see a doctor. Just please don't hassle me. Really. I need time to deal with this. I'm not sure if I ever will.'

'Luke will help you. If you tell him.'

'Tricky when we're no longer seeing each other. Besides, he doesn't want children any more than I do.'

'Nonsense. All men do. They have a built-in desire to replicate themselves.'

'Not Luke,' said Emily, miserably shaking her head.

'Did he tell you that?'

'Yes.'

'Well, he was lying. Or else suffering from some sort of internal trauma.'

'Would still being in love with his wife count as internal trauma?'

'His *wife*?'

'That's what his mother-in-law told me.'

'Whoa!' cried Anna, shaking her head and throwing her

hands in the air. 'Luke's *married*? He has a *mother-in-law*? You've *met* her? Backtrack.'

'Only if you promise to stop speaking in italics.'

Anna nodded vigorously.

'Luke was married to a paediatrician called Grace. She died in a car accident three years ago, around six months after they'd married, I think.'

Anna looked horrified. 'How tragic.'

'Yes. Apparently she was beautiful and caring and warm and obviously perfect. His mother-in-law said he was still in love with her.'

'Is he?'

'I don't know. Probably.'

'Haven't you asked?'

Emily's jaw dropped. 'Of course I haven't asked.'

'You should. His mother-in-law doesn't know his inner thoughts, does she? And she's probably still grieving.'

'So is Luke.'

'Are you sure?'

She hesitated. She didn't know what she thought any more. 'I don't know. Maybe not. He bought the flat he lives in after Grace's death, and the only photos of her are in a handful of albums.' She paused. 'I think I might be the first person he's slept with in three years.'

Anna raised an eyebrow. 'It sounds like he's through with grieving.'

'So why did he end our fling?'

'No idea, but you should tell him about the baby.'

'You're right. I know you are.'

'You're not going to do it, are you?'

Emily fiddled with her hair. 'I will.'

'You can't carry on pretending it's not happening for ever.'

'I know. I do realise denial isn't the way to sort this out, but at the moment it's a cosy place to be.'

Anna glared at her. 'I'm warning you—if you don't tell him soon, then I will. Denial is a complete waste of time.'

Emily let out a sceptical laugh. 'How would you know? You tackle everything head-on.'

'I know all about denial.'

'How?'

'My first two years of art college I spent in denial.'

Emily frowned. 'Really? But you loved it.'

'I hated it.' Anna took a sip of wine.

Emily gaped. 'You *hated* it?'

Anna nodded. 'It was something I'd always thought I wanted to do, but when it came down to it I was bored as hell. All that contemplation and light and depth and perspective. I realised about a week after starting that I'd made the wrong decision. But I couldn't admit defeat. Imagine having to admit to yourself, not to mention to friends, that you have a secret hankering to be an accountant.'

Emily could scarcely believe what she was hearing. 'I thought you took up accountancy because of me.'

'Well, that was part of it. Timing, really. It was the push I needed to take the plunge.'

Emily was pole-axed. Why had they never discussed this before?

'I thought you knew.'

She shook her head. 'I always thought I'd made you sacrifice something you loved.'

Anna gave her a gentle smile. 'Silly thing.'

Emily blinked, trying to come to terms with this new, upside-down world in which years of guilt had just been brushed away as 'silly'. She stared at the twins and her heart felt strangely light. Her hand fell to her abdomen. 'Aren't they gorgeous?' she murmured.

'Do you want to hold one?'

'Would you let me?'

Anna's eyes were shimmering. 'Of course. I've been waiting for ages.'

* * *

The insistent ringing of the doorbell dragged Emily from her shed and had her marching into the house with her hands over her ears and a scowl on her face. Why couldn't she just be left alone? Hadn't whoever it was ever heard of patience?

The Luke-shaped shadow on the other side of the glass made her jerk to a halt in the hall. Her pulse leapt and hope rushed through her. Why was he here? Had he changed his mind? Had he come to apologise? Had he come to confess that he'd been on mind-altering medication and that he was in fact utterly besotted by her?

Stupid fool, she told herself, as the pain he'd caused her flooded back. Bastard. If she slunk into the kitchen would he give up and go away?

'Open the door, Emily. I can see you through the glass.'

Damn. She stood there vacillating for a second, then strode forward and flung the door open.

Luke's eyes were cold, and his face was dark and angry, but nevertheless her heart—pathetically weak organ that it was—squeezed at the sight of him.

'What do you want?'

'When were you going to tell me?'

Emily mentally cursed her meddlesome sister with every filthy word she knew. No point in pretending she didn't know what he was talking about. 'I wasn't.' She tried to shut the door, but he jammed his foot in the gap and then pushed his way into her house.

'Nice of you,' he said grimly.

'Do come in.'

He strode into her sitting room and planted himself in front of the bay window, crossing his arms over his chest. 'When did you find out?'

With the evening sun behind him he looked big and dark, and a shiver of longing ripped through her. Silently cursing her treacherous body, she injected some much needed steel into her spine. 'Three days ago.'

'How did it happen?'

She bristled. 'Do you want me to draw you a picture?'

He glowered at her. 'We were careful. We used condoms every time.'

Emily threw up her hands. 'Well, maybe condoms and hot tubs don't go together. Maybe they weren't within their use-by date. Maybe one split. They're not infallible. Who knows?'

'Maybe you do.'

Emily froze. 'What's that supposed to mean?'

'You tell me.'

'You don't honestly think I've been going round sticking pins in them or something, do you?'

He raised an eyebrow and Emily's blood pressure rocketed. 'How dare you? I'm no more thrilled about this than you are. Have you *ever* listened to anything I've said? I don't want babies. Never have, never will.'

Luke's expression turned even colder and Emily's stomach tensed. 'Of course you don't. In fact with your fear of responsibility, of taking a risk, of actually doing something permanent with your life, I'm surprised you're going through with the pregnancy at all.'

Emily gasped. His words had hit her so hard that she was winded. The air thickened.

Luke shoved his hands through his hair. 'I'm sorry,' he said, 'that was uncalled for.'

'I think you'd better leave.'

'No.'

'Yes.'

'I'm not leaving you in this state.'

'It's your fault I'm in this state. Mental and physical,' she said, clenching her fists. 'You have no right to barge in here, hurling accusations around the place. We are over, remember?'

'That's no excuse.'

'I don't need an excuse. Why are you so angry?'

'You're pregnant with my child—'

'What makes you think it's yours?'

Luke's lips thinned into a tight line. His face turned thunderous.

'OK, it's yours,' she said grudgingly. 'Of course it's yours. I haven't slept with anyone else in over a year.'

'I have a right to know, and you denied me that right.'

'What did you expect me to do?' she said scathingly. 'Place an ad in the *Financial Times*? E-mail you? Turn up on your doorstep? Rather outside the boundaries of our terminated commitment-free relationship, don't you think?'

'You could have rung.'

'Would you have answered my calls?'

'Of course I would have. Don't be ridiculous.' But he didn't look at her, and she felt a surge of righteous satisfaction. 'Why weren't you going to tell me?'

Emily ran a hand through her hair and chewed on her lip. The fact that they'd broken up wasn't really a good excuse, and she couldn't avoid answering him indefinitely.

She stuck her chin up. 'I'll tell you why I didn't tell you if you tell me why you decided to end our fling.'

His eyes glittered at her. 'Agreed. You go first.'

She studied the clock on the mantelpiece. 'The reason I wasn't going to tell you was because I can barely admit it to myself. I was in denial. Probably still am. Is that good enough?'

'Getting there. Why are you in denial?'

'That's none of your business.'

'Oh, I think it very much is.'

Luke still hadn't moved. His eyes fixed on her and she fought the urge to squirm.

'Babies have never been part of my life plan.'

'Why not?'

Emily felt her hackles rise. Hadn't she told him enough that night they'd spent at Anna's house? What did he want? The whole gory story? Well, fine. If he was going to stand there all intimidating and dominating, he could have it.

'Why do you think?' she flung at him. 'I was responsible for the death of my mother. And consequently my father. I ruined my sister's life. I destroyed a perfectly good family. I don't deserve to have one of my own.'

Luke went very still. 'Who told you that?'

'No one. I worked it out all by myself a long time ago.'

'Do you really believe it?'

Emily sank onto the sofa and rubbed her eyes. 'Possibly.' For a long time she had, but her convictions had been on shaky ground even before her conversation with Anna. In fact everything she'd ever believed now seemed to be crumbling around her.

'Is that all there is to it?'

'Isn't that enough?'

Luke frowned. 'I don't think so. I think deep down you *know* you're not responsible for what happened to your family.'

Something inside her snapped. She was fed up with his prodding at her psyche. Fed up with her body's reaction, the constant lurching of her heart and rampaging hormones, and utterly fed up with the futility of being in love with him. She jumped to her feet and glared at him. 'Fine. You want to know what really terrifies me about the whole pregnancy thing?'

He met her challenge with steady eyes.

'Suppose having a child kills me too?'

It was as if someone had hit the pause button. Silence echoed around them. His face softened and his eyes lost some of their iciness. 'Is there any reason it would?'

'The doctor says there isn't, but do you think reason comes into this? My mother had no symptoms. Nothing. She just collapsed the day after she had me. Just like that.' She snapped her fingers.

He unfolded his arms and walked towards her. She just knew he was going to wrap his arms around her and she didn't think she could stand it. 'No,' she said sharply, holding up a hand to ward him off. 'Don't touch me. I should never have let you anywhere near me in the first place.'

Luke recoiled as if she'd hit him, and the shutters came down over his features. He stepped back and turned to look out of the window. 'Is that how you really feel about it?'

Emily went silent. How *did* she feel about it? Denial was no longer an option. She forced herself to think about the tiny life she had inside her. Luke's child. Her heart tripped and then something inside her chest blossomed. There it was again. That spark of sheer joy. Stronger than before. Strong enough to keep burning through the fear. She could do it. Especially if she had Luke by her side. He'd keep her safe. Unlike Tom.

Emily's heart skipped a beat. Where had that thought sprung from? Had she never felt truly safe with Tom? Was that why the not-having-children thing had got so big and so out of control in their relationship? Because she hadn't felt safe enough to overcome her fears? Because their relationship hadn't been solid enough? Because, ultimately, she hadn't loved him enough to give him the one thing he'd wanted?

'I don't know,' she managed, as another long-held belief came crashing down. 'How do you feel about it?'

Luke rubbed a hand over his jaw and his face darkened. 'It's not ideal.'

Emily winced as her insides wrenched. How did he have such power to hurt her?

'Did you really think I wouldn't find out?' he said flatly.

'Why would you? You called a halt to our affair and we don't exactly move in the same circles.'

'As I remember it, you broke up with me.'

'I may have said the words, but that was just timing. I wanted to pre-empt your excuses. Now it's your turn. What reasons were you going to give me for why you decided to break us up?'

He sighed and pushed a hand through his hair.

'Please don't tell me you were going to haul out the "it's not you, it's me" line.'

'Actually, I was going to say it was you.'

Emily's stomach churned. 'Gallant.'

'I would have told you that you're a blonde and I go for brunettes.'

He had been going to reduce it to *hair colour*? Emily

flushed. 'I didn't think you'd had a type in the last three years,' she said bitingly.

Luke tensed, but he carried on as if she hadn't spoken. 'And that you were cathartic. You served a purpose.'

She didn't want to know, but couldn't not ask. 'What sort of purpose?'

'Three years is a long time for any man. You were in the right place at the right time.' She gasped. 'That's what I would have said if you'd asked me why.'

Emily swallowed and tried to stop herself from trembling. 'I wouldn't have let you get away with that.'

'I can't imagine you would have. So what would you have done?'

Luke was still staring out of the window, which made his question easier to answer. Emily took a deep breath. 'After probably slapping you, I'd have called you a coward. I'd have reminded you that you hadn't been to a wedding since your wife died but you went to one with me. You hadn't been to that ball in three years but you took me. When I had heatstroke you could easily have called Anna but you didn't. You stayed and looked after me. You didn't have to help when Charlie was ill but you did. You've been on countless dates since Grace died but you slept with me. You lost control with *me*. I would have told you that I didn't believe all that nonsense about catharsis and hair colour.'

By the time she was finished she was breathing hard and almost bursting with emotion. Luke wasn't saying anything, and he hadn't moved a muscle, so she threw caution to the winds, wanting the truth, however much it hurt.

'Are you still in love with her?'

Luke's jaw clenched and for an awful second Emily thought he might not answer. Then, he said, 'I'll always love her. But, no, I'm not in love with her any more. Not in the way you mean.'

Hope began to bubble inside her and she just couldn't get rid of it. 'So what were your real reasons for ending our affair?'

He turned round slowly, his eyes blank and his expression unreadable. 'You made me feel things I didn't want to feel. You asked for too much. You made me lose control.'

'You can't tell yourself not to feel.'

'Yes, you can.'

She took a deep breath. 'I can't.' She saw him tense and nearly crumbled. But this was her last chance. 'You must know how I feel about you.'

He frowned. 'I warned you.'

His withdrawal was palpable and she felt pain rip through her. What had she been expecting? Luke to fall into her arms, tell her she was right and confess that he loved her too?

She sighed. 'I know you did, Luke, but unfortunately my heart seems to have ignored that particular piece of advice. I'm irreversibly in love with you. I apologise wholeheartedly, but there's nothing I can do about it.'

'There's nothing I can do about it either, Emily,' he said flatly.

Suddenly she'd had enough. Frustration and hurt and hopelessness tangled into one tight ball inside her and she marched up to him.

'You say you're a risk taker. And maybe you are—professionally. But here?' She tapped his chest. 'You're scared.'

His eyes narrowed. 'Quite the psychiatrist.'

His face was hard, empty, and at that moment she hated him. She'd never get through that wall of ice he'd wrapped around his heart. 'Quite the bastard,' she said quietly, backing away on very unsteady legs. She was about to crack open. Her heart was shattering and she was beginning to shake violently.

'You can, of course, see the baby whenever you want, but for the moment I'd like you to go.'

Luke nodded briefly and went.

CHAPTER FOURTEEN

·

LUKE rubbed a weary hand over his face and stared blankly out of the window. The last two weeks had been horrendous. How long had it been since he'd slept properly? Eaten properly? Functioned properly?

He scowled and raked a hand though his hair. He'd done the right thing, walking away from Emily. Saved himself one hell of a lot of pain. He'd just have to keep reminding himself of the fact. More often than he already was. This strange churning inside him would eventually settle. Memories of her would stop filling every corner of his head. The look on her face just before he'd left would eventually stop haunting him. With time. Everything got better with time.

If only he could get rid of the knowledge that by trying to protect himself he'd badly hurt her. And if only he could get rid of the uncomfortable awareness that he'd left her to deal with her pregnancy alone and terrified. Because what was right about that?

The sharp rap on his door jerked him out of his thoughts. 'Come in.' The words came out more harshly than he'd intended, but that seemed to be the norm lately.

He turned to see his secretary standing there, chin up and an unfamiliar determined glare in her eye.

'What is it?' he snapped, and then frowned as shock at his tone registered in her expression.

'Luke, I've been with you now for—what?—five years?'

He nodded curtly and strode across his office to lean back against the edge of his desk. If his extremely well-paid secretary was about to ask for a rise, she could forget it.

'Do you mind if I speak frankly?' she said, marching over to him.

He crossed his arms. 'Please do.'

'I think you should go home.'

He could feel himself glowering at her but couldn't stop it. 'Do you?'

She nodded. 'Or at least go for a walk. Get some air. You've barely left this office in the last fortnight.'

'The company doesn't run itself.'

'At the moment it's a miracle it's making a profit at all.'

He had to keep his mouth clamped tight shut to stop himself from snapping that it was none of her business.

'The only reason no one's said anything is they're terrified you're going to fire them, and the mood you're in I don't blame them.'

Luke ground his teeth. 'Really?'

'Really. This has always been a great place to work, but right now it's horrible.'

His jaw tightened. He didn't trust himself to speak.

His secretary frowned and her expression turned to one of uncertainty. 'Right, well. It had to be said. I'm going home now. You should too. See you tomorrow.'

Luke nodded and rubbed his jaw, which was now hurting with the effort of keeping himself together. Once she'd closed the door behind her with a soft click he let out a long ragged breath. She was right. He was falling apart. Cracking up. Putting the fear of God into everyone around him. Scaring the living daylights out of himself.

Blocking everything out by burying himself in work might have got him through the aftermath of Grace's death, but it wasn't working this time. Not when Emily was out there, living and breathing.

How much longer could he tell himself that his recent lousy run on the markets was simply a case of rotten luck and bad timing?

How much longer could he blame his foul mood and short temper on lack of sleep?

How much longer could he bear the emptiness and the bleakness and the loneliness that wrapped itself round him like a thin grey blanket?

How much longer could he keep up the pretence that he was better off without her?

The fight drained out of him. The fragile barriers around his heart came crashing down and a hundred different emotions flung themselves at him. He nearly collapsed under the onslaught. The sensations whipping around him were so fierce that he had to grip the edge of the desk to keep himself upright.

What the bloody hell was he doing? Or rather not doing? She was out there—the woman who'd offered him her love. The woman he loved.

An amazing woman who'd taken a risk with her pottery and was at this very moment in the middle of one of the most important nights of her life. And here he was, missing her triumph and very possibly throwing away any chance of happiness he had. On the basis of what? The fear of some minuscule probability that, had it cropped up in his work, he would have discounted instantly.

How much longer was he going to carry on being such an almighty idiot?

His heart pounded. He glanced at his watch. Seven thirty. He might just be able to make it. He grabbed his coat and keys and raced out of the office.

Emily gazed round the gallery and tried to muster some enthusiasm. The opening night of her exhibition was a success. The trendy East London gallery was full of glamorous people drinking champagne, eating canapés and actually buying her work—despite Anna adding a zero to her prices. She ought to be bursting with pride, not wafting about listlessly, with her wretchedness hanging over her like a great black cloud.

Her pots and bowls and vases stood on shelves beneath spotlights, each piece shimmering and alive, a cruelly ironic contrast to the feelings swirling about inside her. She heard the roar of a car outside. Another of Anna's well-heeled friends, no doubt. Her heart sank. She wasn't sure she could manage much more of playing the gracious host. There was only one man she really wanted to see and he wasn't here.

So much for her foolish notion that Luke simply needed more time. That not having her around would make him see what he'd given up. And so much for thinking that he would at least step up to his responsibilities. How many times in the last couple of weeks had she envisaged scenarios in which Luke turned up on her doorstep, offering to look after her and the baby? She was pathetic.

A lump lodged in her throat and her eyes stung. She blinked quickly, took a deep breath and fixed a brittle smile to her face.

'Anna, I can't thank you enough for this.'

Anna shrugged. 'I never apologised for getting you into this mess.'

'It's not your fault.'

'I'd give anything to go back and change things.'

'Yes, well, what doesn't kill you makes you stronger.' Not knowing how Luke was or what he was doing wasn't making her stronger. It was slowly and torturously killing her. But she had to face facts. All the time in the universe wouldn't be enough to break down that wall of ice around his heart. The fact that she might not have been the right woman to break through his defences was not something she was going to consider.

'It's a shame you decided not to exhibit that bust. I understand, of course, but it is amazing.'

Emily had finally been unable to prevent herself from sticking together all those Luke-shaped pieces of clay and creating a model of his head. Her heart had ached as she'd moulded his cheekbones, his jaw, the straight nose. She hadn't had to add much water. Her tears had kept the clay perfectly wet.

'I can't bear it. I'm going to have to get rid—'

'You'd better not be talking about me,' said a smooth, deep voice behind her.

Emily's heart stopped and she dropped her glass. The blood roared into her ears. The colour and noise of the gallery disappeared. Her head went dizzy and she swayed. Then her heart started up again, so hard and fast that she thought it would break free. Was she imagining things? No, the wary expression on Anna's face told her everything. Luke was here. He was actually here. Why?

She held herself firm and turned round slowly. He looked as though he'd come straight from work. His suit was immaculate and his shirt was creaseless. But his face was pale and drawn, even though his eyes blazed. Emily nearly stumbled at the look in their depths. What was it? It looked like… No, she thought fiercely. No more self-delusion. No more hoping to find something that wasn't there.

'Lucky you weren't holding one of your pots.' He glanced round the room. 'This is extraordinary.'

She blinked and gave him a cool smile. 'Yes, well, it turns out extreme emotion is good for the creative spirit. But you wouldn't know much about extreme emotion, would you?'

'You'd be surprised.'

The smile that curved his mouth made her mad. How dared he laugh at her? 'What are you doing here?' she demanded.

'I received an invitation.'

'Did you send him an invitation?' said Emily, swinging round to glare at Anna.

Anna's gaze slid to her left. 'I might have done. God, I don't know. I just sent an e-mail to everyone in my address book.'

'Anna…'

'All right, maybe I did. But as soon as I'd sent it I wished I hadn't. OK?'

'Someone wants one of your little red dots,' said Luke.

He waited until Anna had excused herself and dashed off in the direction of a potential customer, and then he turned his full attention back to Emily. Beautiful, incredible Emily. Who'd shaken him up, made him want to live life again, who had one hell of a talent and who was currently taking an unnaturally intense interest in her shoes.

'What were you planning to get rid of?'

Emily flushed. 'Oh, er... My first kiln. It's falling to pieces.'

'Not the baby?'

Her head shot up and she gasped. 'Of course not. Didn't you get the scans I sent?'

'Yes.' He grabbed her arm and pulled her away from the crowds and into an office at the back.

Emily shook herself free and glared at him. 'Hey, I'm the star of the show. And you don't get to manhandle me any more.'

He took a step back as a mixture of pride, admiration, desire and love walloped him in the chest. How had he ever thought he could live without her? 'For someone who's apparently in love with me, you're not being very friendly.'

Her cheeks went pink and she bit on her lip. 'Yeah, well, I'll get over it.'

Luke's heart began to thud loudly. He probably deserved that. But, God, he hoped he hadn't left it too late. His mouth went dry. 'Don't.'

'Don't what?' She looked at him with wary defiance.

'Get over it.'

'Why not?'

'I don't want you to.'

She crossed her arms and lifted her chin. 'Tough. If you can repress your emotions, I'm sure I can.'

Luke thrust his hands into the pockets of his trousers. 'I can't. And let me tell you I've been trying pretty hard. Nice dress, by the way.' She was wearing the midnight-blue dress she'd worn to the gala.

She plucked at the material and frowned. 'I was going to take the shears to it, but it was expensive.'

'So you cut it off at the knees instead.'

'Symbolic, I thought.'

'Whatever the length, I have a sapphire necklace that would look great with it.'

Her eyebrows shot up. 'You bought it? I thought only a fool would do something like that.'

Luke didn't take his eyes off her. 'I'm a fool.'

She sniffed. 'In so many ways.'

He took a deep breath and his heart pounded. 'In particular for being unable to admit to myself just how much I love you.'

For a moment he didn't think she'd heard him. Then her eyes lit up for a split second, and it made him want to punch the air.

'What took you so long?' she said coolly.

'Stubbornness, mainly. With a dose of idiocy and fear thrown in for good measure.'

She bit on her lip and nodded.

His gaze dipped to her mouth. He wanted to haul her into his arms and kiss her senseless. He'd missed her so much. 'You were right,' he said gruffly.

'About what?'

'Everything. The way you make me feel scares the hell out of me. And the idea of ever losing you terrifies me. But not having you with me is far, far worse.'

'So where have you been?'

'Hell and back.'

'Good.'

'In a Zonda.'

'Am I supposed to be impressed?'

'Yes.'

'Even if I knew what it was, I doubt I would be.'

'It's a very fast sports car. I bought it last week. I used to have one years ago. It's sitting outside.'

'I hope it gets towed.' She studied her nails. 'Most men when they're about to become fathers trade in the sports car.'

'True, but our whole relationship has been the wrong way round.'

'I wasn't aware we *had* a relationship.'

Luke's eyes narrowed. 'You're deliberately making me suffer, aren't you?' Surely this was a good sign. Wasn't it? If she didn't still feel something for him she wouldn't still be here, would she?

'Don't you think I'm entitled to?'

'You said you were irreversibly in love with me.'

Emily frowned. 'Lately I've been reconsidering the irreversible bit.'

A chill ran through him. 'And?'

'I'm still thinking.'

'Well, while you are, let me tell you what made me realise I couldn't carry on denying how I felt about you.'

'What makes you think I'm interested?'

'You will be. It was your vase.'

That captured her attention. She stared at him. 'My vase?'

'Mmm. There it was, lurking in the corner of my sitting room—'

She shot him a furious look. 'My pottery does not lurk.'

'You're quite right. It doesn't. Your pottery is bright and vibrant. In fact it's pretty amazing.'

'My vase brought warmth and colour into an otherwise sterile environment.'

'Exactly. But I quite liked my safe, sterile environment. And I didn't like the vase reminding me of you, so I put it in a cupboard.'

'That's cruel.'

Luke nodded. 'Unfortunately it left a gap where it should have been. And there's a gap here too.' He tapped his chest. 'Where you should be.' Emily went very still. 'I lose control when you're around and I like it. I only sleep well when I sleep with you. I need you, Emily, and I love you.'

'You've made me pretty miserable.'

The look in her eyes made his heart wrench. 'I know.' His gut clenched with regret. 'I'm so very sorry.'

'This pregnancy thing is hard to do alone.'

'You don't have to. I won't let anything happen to you. If you marry me, I'll spend the rest of my life making sure of it.'

She didn't answer, and Luke suddenly knew what real fear felt like. It clawed away at him. Had he blown it? He went very cold at the thought that Emily didn't love him, didn't want him. That he'd killed any feelings she'd had for him. The need to know either way burned inside him. 'How's that thought process coming along?' His voice cracked and he cleared his throat.

'All done.'

He saw the ghost of a smile hover over her mouth and he suddenly remembered how to breathe. 'And?' He scanned her features, but they held no indication of what was going through her mind.

'It seems irreversible is about right,' she said.

What the hell did *that* mean? Luke was about to demand clarification, but then her eyes met his and he felt himself quake.

She walked up to him and wound her arms around his neck. 'I've tried so hard to stop loving you, but I can't.'

His heart lurched violently and relief poured through him. 'Thank God,' he murmured, wrapping his arms around her and crushing her against him. 'Marry me.'

She pulled back and looked up at him, happiness spreading across her face like sunshine. 'Are you sure?'

He was never letting her out of his sight again. 'You're having my baby.'

'Good point,' she said softly.

His eyes blazed down at her. 'How are you feeling about that?'

'I want it with a fierceness that scares me. You?'

'Unexpectedly ecstatic. I love you so very much.' He looked deep into her eyes and his throat clogged.

'I love you too. We're going to be fine, aren't we?' she murmured, putting her hand on his chest where his heart racing.

'We're going to be so much better than fine,' he said, lowering his mouth to hers and kissing her until they were both shaking. 'I promise.'

PREGNANT BRIDES

*Inexperienced and expecting,
they're forced to marry!*

Bestselling Harlequin Presents author

Lynne Graham

brings you the second story
in this exciting new trilogy:

RUTHLESS MAGNATE,
CONVENIENT WIFE
#2892
Available February 2010

Also look for

GREEK TYCOON,
INEXPERIENCED MISTRESS
#2900
Available March 2010

HARLEQUIN *Presents*

TWO CROWNS, TWO ISLANDS, ONE LEGACY

A royal family torn apart by pride and its lust for power, reunited by purity and passion

THE ROYAL HOUSE *of* KAREDES

Harlequin Presents is proud to bring you the final installment from The Royal House of Karedes. As the stories unfold, secrets and sins from the past are revealed and desire, love and passion war with royal duty!

Look for:

THE DESERT KING'S HOUSEKEEPER BRIDE
#2891

by Carol Marinelli
February 2010

REQUEST YOUR FREE BOOKS!

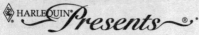 HARLEQUIN *Presents*

PASSION
GUARANTEED
SEDUCTION

2 FREE NOVELS PLUS 2 FREE GIFTS!

YES! Please send me 2 FREE Harlequin Presents® novels and my 2 FREE gifts (gifts are worth about $10). After receiving them, if I don't wish to receive any more books, I can return the shipping statement marked "cancel". If I don't cancel, I will receive 6 brand-new novels every month and be billed just $4.05 per book in the U.S. or $4.74 per book in Canada. That's a savings of close to 15% off the cover price! It's quite a bargain! Shipping and handling is just 50¢ per book*. I understand that accepting the 2 free books and gifts places me under no obligation to buy anything. I can always return a shipment and cancel at any time. Even if I never buy another book, the two free books and gifts are mine to keep forever.   106 HDN EYRQ 306 HDN EYR2

Name   (PLEASE PRINT)

Address   Apt. #

City   State/Prov.   Zip/Postal Code

Signature (if under 18, a parent or guardian must sign)

Mail to the **Harlequin Reader Service:**
IN U.S.A.: P.O. Box 1867, Buffalo, NY 14240-1867
IN CANADA: P.O. Box 609, Fort Erie, Ontario L2A 5X3

Not valid to current subscribers of Harlequin Presents books.

Are you a current subscriber of Harlequin Presents books and want to receive the larger-print edition? Call 1-800-873-8635 today!

* Terms and prices subject to change without notice. Prices do not include applicable taxes. Sales tax applicable in N.Y. Canadian residents will be charged applicable provincial taxes and GST. Offer not valid in Quebec. This offer is limited to one order per household. All orders subject to approval. Credit or debit balances in a customer's account(s) may be offset by any other outstanding balance owed by or to the customer. Please allow 4 to 6 weeks for delivery. Offer available while quantities last.

Your Privacy: Harlequin Books is committed to protecting your privacy. Our Privacy Policy is available online at www.eHarlequin.com or upon request from the Reader Service. From time to time we make our lists of customers available to reputable third parties who may have a product or service of interest to you. If you would prefer we not share your name and address, please check here. ☐

HARLEQUIN
Ambassadors

Want to share your passion for reading Harlequin® Books?

Become a Harlequin Ambassador!

Harlequin Ambassadors are a group of passionate and well-connected readers who are willing to share their joy of reading Harlequin® books with family and friends.

You'll be sent all the tools you need to spark great conversation, including free books!

All we ask is that you share the romance with your friends and family!

You'll also be invited to have a say in new book ideas and exchange opinions with women just like you!

To see if you qualify* to be a Harlequin Ambassador, please visit www.HarlequinAmbassadors.com.

*Please note that not everyone who applies to be a Harlequin Ambassador will qualify. For more information please visit www.HarlequinAmbassadors.com.

Thank you for your participation.

BAP09BPA